# The Summer Wedding Murder

David W. Robinson

Discover us online:
**www.crookedcatpublishing.com**

Join us on facebook:
**www.facebook.com/crookedcatpublishing**

Tweet a photo of yourself holding
this book to **@crookedcatbooks**
and something nice will happen.

# The Author

David Robinson is a Yorkshireman living on the outskirts of Manchester, northwest England, with his wife and a crazy Jack Russell Terrier named Joe (because he looks like a Joe).

David writes in several genres under different pseudonyms, but his mainstay is crime and mystery. In January 2012 Crooked Cat Publishing picked up the first of his popular Sanford 3rd Age Club Mysteries, The Filey Connection. Since then a further seven STAC Mysteries have been published by Crooked Cat, more titles are planned for 2013 and 2014.

He also produces darker, edgier thrillers, such as The Handshaker and Voices; titles which are aimed exclusively at an adult audience and which question our perceptions of reality.

As at June 2013, he is working on the ninth STAC Mystery, Costa del Murder, and the first of a new series with amateur sleuth, Maddy Chester.

**Website and blog** http://www.dwrob.com
**email:** dwrob96@gmail.com

## By the same author

The STAC Mystery series:

The Filey Connection

The I-Spy Murders

A Halloween Homicide

A Murder for Christmas

Murder at the Murder Mystery Weekend

My Deadly Valentine

The Chocolate Egg Murders

The Summer Wedding Murder

Costa del Murder

Other work:

Voices

The Handshaker

# The Summer Wedding Murder

## A Sanford 3rd Age Club Mystery
## David W Robinson

Read the first chapter of the next STAC Mystery,
Costa del Murder, at the end of this story.

# Chapter One

Joe Murray shook his head sadly. "Fifty years and more this café has stood here. And in all that time, it's never been shut on a weekday or a Saturday. Over half a century, and apart from Sundays, that door has never been shut." He nodded beyond the queue of customers, to the entrance of the Lazy Luncheonette.

"It was closed for your mother's funeral," Len, the drayman on the other side of the counter pointed out.

Joe pushed a beaker of tea to him, and took his money. "One full English, one beaker of tea, that's six fifty to you." He rang up the money, dropped the ten pound note in the till, and handed over the change. "There you go, Len. And, by the way, you're wrong. It was only shut for half a day when me old queen was buried. The service wasn't until two in the afternoon, and I was open until dinner time. It was the same when the old man died."

Half past seven on a Thursday morning, and the Lazy Luncheonette was packed with the drivers and mates from the Sanford Brewery. Outside, the sun shone on gridlocked, rush hour traffic, and the heat of a glorious June morning compounded the frustration of drivers in a reluctant hurry to get to work. And while they sat, they feasted envious eyes on the free-flowing traffic coming away from the town on this side of the dual carriageway.

No one could ever accuse Joe of inaccuracy. Whether as Alf's Café, Joe's Café or The Lazy Luncheonette, the place had stood in the centre of Britannia Parade (a cutting off the side

3

of Doncaster Road) since the end of World War Two, its doors always open. In the days of the pit and foundry, it had catered for the lorry drivers trundling to and fro. With the passing of the old economy, it turned its attention to the mechanics and apprentices from the engineering factories on the other side of the dual carriageway, and the shoppers from Sanford Retail Park at the rear. The draymen of Sanford Brewery, who supplied the town's pubs and clubs, had long been the most faithful supporters of the place in all its incarnations.

Inside the café, notwithstanding the early hour, the heat had reached levels which were almost intolerable, and Joe had positioned three free-standing fans in the dining area, while Brenda Jump had commandeered a fourth for the kitchen.

"I have the door open," she had told Joe, "but there's no breeze and it's hot as hell in here."

The draymen were usually distinguished by their pale green uniforms, but the weather called for T-shirts, and some of them, including Len and his mate, Barry, had abandoned their trousers for shorts. Joe envied them. Food hygiene regulations meant he had to be properly dressed at all times, and the risk of scalds and burns from hot appliances in the kitchen and around the counter area, effectively excluded the wearing of shorts.

While handing over Len's change, he scanned the dining area, packed with customers, mainly draymen, with a few passing lorry drivers, and one or two employees of the factories opposite.

A table of draymen had one of his casebooks open as they ate. Joe vented his irritation on them. "Hey, you lot. Don't get brown sauce and fried tomatoes over that book or I'll bill you for reprinting."

"Just checking what you were up to in Weston-super-Mare, Joe," one of them called back.

"The case of The Chocolate Egg Killer," said another and the table dissolved into laughter.

The waiting queue shuffled forward as Len, laughing at the chocolate egg joke, wandered away, and his mate, Barry, stepped up to the counter. "Same again, Joe," he ordered.

"One full English and mug of tea." Joe made out the note, passed it through the hatch to the kitchen and poured the tea.

"What about when Lee got married?" Barry asked. "You musta shut down then."

"He got married at three o'clock on a Saturday afternoon," Joe replied, "and it was business as normal for the morning." Again he pushed the tea across the counter, and took the money. "But tomorrow, it's not business as normal. I wouldn't care, but it's not as if Wes Staines is family."

Barry frowned. "Wes Staines? Alec's lad? You're off to his wedding? I thought he lived somewhere up in the Lake District."

"He does. Windermere. We have to travel all that way to see the silly sod sign his life away."

Barry chuckled. "It's not compulsory, is it?"

Sheila Riley danced out of the kitchen carrying four meals. "Yes it is. And that's why old misery guts has to shut up shop tomorrow, and we won't open again until Monday morning."

Barry picked up his tea. "I thought your Lee looked after the place when you're away."

Lee, the genial giant of the Lazy Luncheonette kitchen, appeared in the doorway, his chef's hat tipped at an odd angle. "Wes is a mate of mine, Barry. I got an invite. Uncle Joe is only going cos Alec Staines wanted him there."

Barry laughed again. "Why, is he expecting a murder?"

Joe frowned. "No. He's lending me an alibi for the case of the murdered drayman. Now push off so I can serve your pals."

Ever since the wedding invitations first went out in April, and he realised the implications for the Lazy Luncheonette, Joe had sought ways and means of getting round the problem, right down to flatly refusing to attend.

"Alec is one of your oldest friends, Joe," Sheila had reminded him, "and he and Julia are stalwarts of the 3rd Age Club. You can't let them down."

Joe had switched his attention to the more malleable Lee. A huge young man, a former prop forward for the Sanford Bulls rugby league team, an excellent cook and the closest Joe had to family, he had never been blessed with the sharpest mind. Joe had been well on the way to persuading Lee that he would not enjoy a couple of days in the Lake District when Cheryl, Lee's wife, stepped in.

"Wes played for the Sanford Bulls, too, Uncle Joe. Him and Lee were good mates. He has to be there, and you ought to be ashamed of yourself, trying to talk him out of it just for the sake of the café."

With this in mind, Joe handed Barry his change, and said, "It's not the café I'm bothered about. It's you lads. You've been coming here for years. You expect us to be open. What will you do for breakfast on Friday and Saturday?"

Barry looked glumly at his change. "Go to Sid's Caff on the by-pass. Maybe I'll get more mileage outta me tenner there."

"Yeah. And you'll be able to spend your extra money on dental work. I'm told his sausages are like concrete." Joe dismissed Barry and concentrated on the next customer, another drayman. "Whaddya want?"

"That's why we all come here, Joe. No one can beat you when it comes to social niceties like saying 'good morning'."

"If you don't like it here sod off to Sid's Caff and suffer his sausages."

Scurrying back to the kitchen, laden with dirty plates, cups and cutlery, Sheila said, "I'm surprised you could get all those esses out without losing your dentures."

\*\*\*

Joe could be found at table five, the one nearest the

6

counter, no later than 10.30am every morning.

"I've been a fixture in this place so long there's nothing you can tell me about it that I don't already know, including when there'll be a lull lasting long enough for me to take a break."

Under normal circumstances, he would pass the time with the cryptic crossword in the *Daily Express*, but the prospect of Windermere and the comparative horror the Lazy Luncheonette closing for two days, preoccupied him as he carried a beaker of tea to the table and took his seat with Sheila and Brenda, basking in the cool breeze of a free-standing fan.

"The wedding isn't until two o'clock tomorrow," he announced. "Suppose we opened, dealt with the breakfast crowd, shut the doors at, say, half past ten, then legged it over to Windermere. We could be there in plenty of time."

Sheila tutted. "The wedding is at eleven o'clock tomorrow morning, and we have been invited to attend the ceremony, not just the reception and evening disco."

Joe sighed. "I don't want to set a precedent."

Brenda, who had only just returned from delivering the sandwich order to Ingleton Engineering, tutted. "It's time a precedent was set. You're not getting any younger, Joe, and it's high time you learned to shut down for the odd day or two. Relax a little."

"I get plenya relaxation. Lee takes over when I'm not here. It's just that this time—"

Sheila interrupted. "If you're that desperate to have the place opened, how about those people Cheryl brings in when we're away? Her mother, and that friend of hers, Pauline."

Joe shook his head. "I don't mind Mary, Cheryl's ma, and Pauline helping out, but Cheryl is with us this time and I won't leave the job to her mother and her friend. I don't trust them."

"With the café or the money?"

Joe scowled at Brenda. "Either. Both."

"I've told Ingleton's we're shut for the day, Broadbent's and the other factories over the road know about it, the high priced eateries on the Retail Park are cheering because they'll pick up the slack, and the draymen are all aware of it. The only person who isn't dealing with it is you."

The accusation stung Joe into retaliation. "Do you have any idea how much it costs to shut down?" He gestured at the ceiling with both hands. "The taxes, gas, water and electricity bills don't take a day off. The chillers and freezers keep going while we're not here, the insurance doesn't drop for shutting down one day, and I still have you people to pay. And as I keep saying, we don't know how much permanent trade we'll drive away. The draymen might be laughing at having to go to Sid's Caff on the by-pass, but some of 'em might find Sid Snetterton preferable to Joe Murray."

Brenda shook her head. "Can't see it. They get a much better class of insult here."

"Gar." Joe dismissed her with a growl.

"Changing the subject slightly," Brenda went on, "if you're taking us in your car, you need to get it valeted."

Joe's face registered blatant shock. "What?"

"Joe, that car is hanging. Inside and out. When the hell did you last clean it? The Queen's Jubilee?"

"Silver Jubilee, I reckon," Sheila tittered.

"It goes just as fast with the muck on it," Joe protested.

Sheila waded in on Brenda's side. "Probably, but you're going to be wearing your best suit, and we'll be in our Sunday best."

"We spent a lot of money on our outfits, Joe, and you even had your suit cleaned," Brenda reminded him.

"You won't be travelling in them," Joe argued. "We're leaving early. We'll be at the hotel in Windermere in plenty of time to change before we go onto the church."

"Manor House."

"Pardon me?"

"They're getting married at The Lakeside Manor House, not in church," Brenda reiterated.

"Oh, well in that case, we'll have tons of time. We're staying at the same place. Just make sure you wrap your clobber up well, and—"

"Clean the car, Joe, or Brenda and I will travel in mine," Sheila warned him. "That heap of yours has things living in it."

Joe conceded defeat. "I'll do it when I've had this cup of tea."

The doorbell chimed and Alec Staines entered.

Any other working day would find Alec dressed in his white, painter's overalls, but to their surprise, he was wearing a pair of denim shorts and a scruffy T-shirt bearing the legend 'The King Lives Forever' over a stylised image of Elvis Presley.

Joe moved quickly behind the counter and poured Alec a beaker of tea. "Where are you working today? Glastonbury?"

"Not working, Joe," Alec said, sitting alongside Brenda. "On our way to Windermere this afternoon. Gotta be there in plenty of time for the big do."

"Formal dress, Alec?" Sheila asked.

"Top hat and tails. Morning suit. Grey. Complete with cravat. Wes and his girl went for it, and Julia insisted. Cost me a bleeding fortune, and I felt a right prat when I tried it on at the hire shop."

Placing the beaker in front of Alec, Joe sat with Sheila. "So what you doing here? Slumming?"

"Just checking you're all in the frame and ready to go."

"Everything is just about organised," Brenda replied, "except for his lordship. He's worrying about lost trade."

"You'll get it back, Joe."

"The draymen are on about going to Sid's Caff, tomorrow and Saturday."

Alec laughed. "In that case, you'll definitely get it back. No disrespect to Sid Snetterton, but I wouldn't wash your feet in

9

his tea, never mind my own. Anyway, you've got Lee to…" Alec trailed off. "Oh. Course. Lee and Cheryl are going to Windermere, aren't they?"

At the mention of his name, Lee appeared in the kitchen doorway and grinned. "Looking forward to it, Mr Staines. Me and Wes go way back. School, and then the Sanford Bulls. He were a mean full back, your Wes."

Alec thanked him with a fond smile, then addressed Joe's concerns. "If it's difficult, Joe, I can always make excuses for you. Turning up is not compulsory, you know, but you've known Wes all his life."

Joe was about to seize upon Alec's offer, but Sheila beat him to it.

"It's not difficult, Alec, and Joe doesn't want to miss Wes's wedding. Do you Joe?"

Alec laughed again. "When did you lose your voice, Joe?"

"The day I took these two on." Joe fished into his pocket and came out with a half-smoked cigarette. "Come on. Let's step outside for a cough and spit."

After the movement of air created by the fan, the still, raw heat of the pavement hit them like a hammer blow. Joe felt the sweat breaking on his brow the moment he stepped out.

"You're driving over tomorrow, Joe?" Alec asked as they walked through the door.

"Leaving about half past six in the morning. According to Google maps, it'll take about two hours. We figure we'll be the other side of Manchester before the morning rush really picks up, and even stopping for breakfast, we'll be there for about nine. That gives us time to check in and change." Leaning against the window, he lit his cigarette stub and immediately began to cough violently.

"What the hell are you smoking, Joe?" Alec demanded.

"It's the heat," Joe said, his eyes watering as he struggled to get his breath. "I'll be fine in a minute." He leaned forward and gulped in a lungful of air.

"You'll be all right next week, then," Alec said. "The forecast says it's going to break on Sunday or Monday. Our Wes picked the perfect time to get spliced."

Straightening up, better in control of his breathing, Joe asked, "What's up with your Wes, anyway? Getting married on a Friday. I question the sanity of anyone actually getting married these days, but to do it on a Friday…"

He trailed off and waited for an answer.

Alec, too, lit a cigarette. "You're a cynical old sod, you are. Just cos it didn't work out between you and Alison."

"It's not just because of that."

"There's nowt wrong with marriage, Joe. Look at me and Julia. We've been wed near thirty-five years and I couldn't want for a better wife."

"I reserve the right to disagree," Joe declared. "On the grounds that Alison buggered off and left me. Anyway, I'm not arguing about your marriage… or anyone else's come to that, I'm asking why he's getting married on a Friday."

"Flights."

Joe frowned. "What about them?"

"They're flying to the Maldives for their honeymoon early doors Saturday morning. They have to be at Manchester Airport for stupid o'clock: about half past five in the morning, and it'll take 'em, what, an hour and half to get from Windermere to Manchester. They couldn't have the wedding on a Saturday if they'd wanted." Alec grinned again and finished his tea. Handing the beaker back to Joe, he went on, "Sorry, Joe, but Wes wasn't about to change his plans to accommodate you or the Lazy Luncheonette."

"No, no. Course not. So how long has he known this girl?"

"Kelly? About three years, I reckon. They've been living together for the last two."

"And suddenly decided to waste half their savings on a wedding?" Joe sounded incredulous. "They must have more money than sense. Coining it, is he? Your Wes?"

11

"Making more than I am." Alec nodded. "Him and his mate, Rott. You remember him. Paul Drummond. Him, our Wes and your Lee were big mates when they left school."

"I remember Rott," Joe said, grimly. "Bad tempered so-and-so, wasn't he?"

"That's the Irish in him, Joe. Always was a hothead. That's why they called him Rott. Short for Rottie, as in Rottweiler."

"Ah. Right. He's calmed down a bit, I take it."

"Not so's you'd notice," Alec replied. "Still a snapper. Put a bit of weight on though. Too much beer, not enough weightlifting."

Joe nodded. His problems were the exact opposite: not enough beer and too much exercise chasing after customers and suppliers. "And they're working together?"

Alec blew out a cloud of smoke. "Him and our Wes set up in business together. What with all the holiday places in the Lake District, there's plenty to do during the summer. Repair work and stuff. And off-season, there's a lot of refurbishment work to be done. According to what Wes told me, they could do with another pair of hands, but they can't find anyone dumb enough to work for a nutter like Rott."

"I seem to remember the only ones who could take Rott down on the field were Wes and Lee," Joe said.

"Correct. Wes and Lee were always the more focussed. They were training with the Sanford Bulls, so they kept off the beer. Rott liked his ale too much." Alec laughed and took another pull on his cigarette. "Rott is Wes's best man."

Joe's imagination ran riot with the prospect. "That should be fun. Best man gets tanked up, makes a pass at the bride by mistake and all hell breaks loose. Remind me to duck."

Alec took a final drag on his smoke and crushed it out on the wall-mounted stubber.

"According to my information, Rott has promised to be on his best behaviour, so you shouldn't need to duck. Listen, Joe, I'll have to shoot off, but you know, if it's difficult for you tomorrow. Give it a miss. I'll explain to Wes and it's not like he'll burst into tears. He'll have more on his plate."

"Nah, mate, like the girls said, it's too late now. All the arrangements are made. If I opened the café, no one would turn up. They all know we're shut. Besides, we've booked the hotel for the weekend."

Alec gave him a mock-suspicious gaze. "Oh, aye? You and Brenda in one room, Sheila in another, Joe bedhopping between the two."

Joe laughed. "Chance would be a fine thing."

"I thought you had Brenda sorted."

"Dying off." Joe, too, stubbed out his cigarette as three women ambled along the parade from the direction of the retail park. "It was never anything serious, you know."

"It never is with Brenda, is it?"

Joe refrained from making the obvious comments, and nodded at the three women coming their way. "This lot look like customers. I'll see you in Windermere tomorrow, Alec."

# Chapter Two

With fine views of Lake Windermere through the tree line, The Lakeside Manor Hotel stood on a rise at the end of a narrow, twisting lane, off the main road between Bowness and Windermere.

But as Joe grumpily pointed out, it could hardly be said to be at the side of the lake.

"I wouldn't like to walk it," he grumbled as he climbed out of his car. "It must be nigh on half a mile."

Joe's irritation had been a feature of the journey all the way from Sanford. He had led the way, and eager not to lose Lee, Cheryl and their son, Danny, in their car, Joe had taken it easy across the Pennines and round Manchester. But that had cost them time, and it was 9.30am when he finally pulled into the Lakeside's busy car park.

The heat, too, had added to his displeasure. Dawn had broken just before 5.00am and by the time they left the Lazy Luncheonette just after six thirty, the temperature was already in the low twenties. Reaching the other side of Manchester an hour later, it was climbing towards the thirty mark, and even with the sunroof open, the interior felt like a steam room.

"We've both spent a fortune at the hairdresser's," Sheila said, pooh-poohing his idea of opening all the windows, too. "We don't want it spoiled by hurricanes coming through the windows."

"It might help if you bought a new car," Brenda pointed out. "One with air-conditioning."

"How often do we need air-con in this country? And

besides, have you seen what it does to fuel consumption? You need a bloody petrol tanker following you."

"According to motor manufacturers, the effect is minimal," Sheila said.

"Yes, and according to Sid Snetterton, his sausages are the best in Sanford, but that doesn't make it true. Try reading *What Car* instead of *Hair & Beauty* and you might know what you're talking about."

But in deference to their expensive hairdos, he kept the windows closed and vented his anger on other road users, the worst of his vehemence falling on lorry drivers.

"Not only do I have to serve them six days a week, but when I do get a day off, they're in my way." He whined as two lorries blocked the inner and middle lanes, and heavy traffic prevented him getting into the offside lane to overtake.

The final sixteen miles from leaving the motorway to arriving in Bowness on Windermere, travelling along wooded lanes, with occasional glimpses of the surrounding hills and moors, took the better part of thirty-five minutes, and they were almost in Bowness before they caught their first sight of the lake. By that time, Joe's temper was on the point of eruption.

It was exacerbated by the difficulty in finding the Lakeside Manor. The lane which led to it belonged to the hotel and as a result was badly signposted. Joe passed it twice, once in each direction before Sheila finally spotted it.

It was with some relief that they finally got out of the car, and took the luggage from the rear.

"Sort yourselves out," Joe ordered. "I'll go check us in."

Wearing only a T-shirt, shorts and trainers, he felt the stress leaving him as he walked towards the main entrance. It was, he told himself, always the same. He disliked travelling whether he was driving or not, but he enjoyed arriving.

The Lakeside Manor had been a manor house at one time, built of local stone, its façade recently cleaned, it gave the impression of a miniature castle sitting in a couple of acres of finely manicured lawn and garden. Although Joe could see only part of the surrounding land from the tarmac of the car park, its ordered, yet casual furnishings appealed to him. He had an instant and pleasing vision of sitting by one of the tables enjoying the sun, and watching the boats on the distant lake.

The temporary hiatus to his mood did not last long. He stepped through the main doors, into the lobby's plush interior to find an officious woman, immaculately attired in a dark skirt and pale blue shirt, haranguing a tall man in overalls who carried a small toolbox.

"You use the tradesman's entrance," she barked. "You've been here often enough to know that."

"I'm servicing these phones," the man grumbled, and waved at the telephones on the highly polished counter.

"Nevertheless, you do not walk through those doors and present yourself here," said the receptionist, pointing to the entrance through which Joe had just come. "Now go back out, left, left again, and report to Mr Prosser, our duty maintenance supervisor."

Chuntering audibly but incoherently, the man turned and marched irritably past Joe, who turned to watched him leave, then approached reception.

Her name badge identified her as Harriet Atkinson, Receptionist. Stocky and broad shouldered for a woman, her chubby face reminded Joe of a teacher from his years in primary school; one that would brook no argument or impertinence. Steely eyes impaled him from behind tiny glasses.

"And you are?"

Joe, who had long been used to dealing with irritable customers, was not fazed. "Yes. I am."

Harriet, whom Joe guessed to be about his age, was momentarily perplexed. Recovering her severe composure, she demanded, "Who are you and what do you want?"

"I'm Joe Murray and if you've got a minute, I'd like to check in."

The frown did not recede. "You're a guest?"

"I have three rooms booked. A single for me, a twin for my two friends, Mrs Riley and Mrs Jump, and a double with child bed for my nephew, Lee Murray, his wife and son."

Harriet looked him up and down. "The Lakeside Manor Hotel prefers its guests to be properly dressed at all times."

"And the Lazy Luncheonette prefers its patrons to eat up and get out of the way sharpish, so that others can sit down, but we don't always get our own way."

Joe's irascible announcement created more perplexity. "What?"

"Who's paying the bloody bill?" Joe snapped. "I am. And I'll dress as I see fit. As long as I'm not mooning you, it's no business of yours."

Harriet pointed to a small brass plaque, which declared, *The Lakeside Manor Hotel reserves the right to refuse admission.* "I think you'll find that it is our business, and if you read our brochure, you would see that we stipulate proper attire at all times. Not…" She trailed off and waved vaguely at his shabby clothing. "…tatty shorts, dirty trainers and a grubby shirt."

"Are you booking me in or not, you snooty cow?"

Obviously feeling she had the upper hand, Harriet waved at another sign, a printed notice this time, pinned to the rear wall. *The Lakeside Manor Hotel will not tolerate aggression or abusive behaviour towards its staff.*

"I don't have to put up with that," she told him.

Never one to back down easily, Joe retaliated, "And I don't have to put up with this crap from you. Get the manager out here."

"Mr Nelson doesn't come on duty until one o'clock this afternoon. At this moment, I am in charge."

"So what will you do for an encore? Release the hounds.

Now, are you gonna book me in or not?"

"Dressed like that, I should—"

"No problem," Joe interrupted. "I'll change… on your car park."

Horror spread across Harriet's face. "You can't do that."

"Watch me. And if it's caught on your CCTV, maybe I'll send it in to *You've Been Framed*. The two hundred and fifty quid would just about cover the cost of this weekend." Joe turned to leave, and as he did so, Alec Staines appeared from one of the two lifts.

Dressed in a grey morning suit, white shirt and cravat, his thinning hair slicked down with gel, Joe did not register him until he spoke.

"Hey up, Joe. You made it then?"

It was with a feeling of relief that Joe turned to shake hands. "I almost made it, Alec." He jerked a thumb at Harriet. "Unfortunately, Atilla the Hen here is insisting I get changed, so I'm going to do a strip in the car park. Wanna come and watch?"

"I resent that—"

Alec cut her off. "Ms Atkinson, Joe is with our party."

"We have standards, Mr Staines. And by the way, it's Mrs Atkinson. I'm a married woman."

"Your husband must have serious bottle to climb into the same bed as you."

Joe did not mean to say it. The thought was at the forefront of his mind, and slipped out before he could stop it. His comment sparked another round of bitter recrimination between him and the equally bad-tempered Mrs Atkinson before Alec calmed things down and persuaded her.

"Mrs Atkinson, Joe is one of Sanford's most important businessmen. He's had a long, and I should think a hot and uncomfortable journey. If you let him and his party check in, I'm sure he'll be happy to change once he gets to his room. Isn't that right, Joe?"

"Yeah, yeah. Sure. Whatever you want, Alec."

Mrs Atkinson huffed and puffed. "This is very irregular."

"Old fashioned is what it is," Joe argued. "And I mean your policies, not my dress. Now, can we get on with the job?"

He completed the registration card, handed over his credit card so it could be scanned, and Mrs Atkinson rang the bell on the counter. A moment later, a young man emerged from the room at the far end of the lobby. "Show this gentleman and his party to their rooms. Ten, eleven and twelve."

"Yes, Ms Atkinson." The young man took the keycards from her.

They took the lift up to the first floor where the porter opened each of the three rooms in turn, letting Sheila and Brenda into room ten, Lee, Cheryl and Danny into twelve, and Joe between them at number eleven.

Joe fished into his pocket for a pound coin and handed it over. "There you go, lad."

"Enjoy your stay, sir."

Joe closed the door behind the porter, turned to throw back the curtains and looked out.

That sense of peace, of which he had had an inkling before events in reception, flooded over him again, and this time, it was for real.

His room looked out over the lawns to the side of the hotel, and over the tree line to Lake Windermere, where he could see crowded boats, some small, others not so small, plodding across the blue waters. A path led down the hill towards the high railings and a black, stone wall on the roadside. Further down, it disappeared behind a small copse, and over the treetops, Joe could see the square tower of a small church. Turning slightly to his left, on a narrow angle through the trees, he could see Bowness boat station and queues of people waiting to board the steamers for one of the several trips around and across the lake. Nearer to him, tables and chairs spread on the lawns of the Lakeside Manor were mainly occupied, and in the heart of the lawns stood a giant marquee, its entrance decorated with statues and white planters filled with flowers. The wedding venue, Joe guessed; or perhaps the reception venue.

Thoughts of the wedding prompted him to check his watch. Time was moving on. The fiasco with Ms Atkinson in reception had taken longer than he imagined, and his watch read nearly ten o'clock. He hurriedly unzipped the travel carrier, took out his suit and shirt, and hung them on the wardrobe door. Opening up his suitcase, he removed his shoes and put them beneath the table under the window, then, taking out clean underwear and his shaving/bathing travel bag, he made for the shower.

Twenty minutes later, Room Service delivered a tray of tea while he checked his appearance in the mirror. Pristine, was his opinion. His black tie tucked neatly under his Adam's apple, gold cuff links gleaming in the morning sunlight, crinkly hair brushed into position, he lacked only his jacket to complete the picture of sartorial perfection.

At 10.45am, he met Sheila and Brenda in the bar, and ordered himself a beer.

He eyed the barman's name tag. "Storm. Unusual name."

The young lad, a pencil thin, dark-haired individual, smiled good-naturedly. "You wouldn't believe the grief I got at school."

"You mean it's your real name?"

Storm nodded and Joe's astonishment settled to a cynical yet sympathetic chuckle.

"Parents, eh? They don't always think about the consequences. Why did they give you that name?"

Storm smiled again. "It's all to do with my birthday."

It was obvious he did not want to talk about it, so Joe changed the subject, concentrating on the young man's accent. "You're not from this area originally?"

"No, sir. Londoner. Life's a bit more pleasant in these

parts."

Ordering Storm to add the cost of the drink to his bill, Joe joined his two companions by the exit.

Both women had opted for conservatism over flamboyance, yet chosen colours of summer freshness. Sheila wore a skirt and blouse in pale lemon, Brenda had opted for lively, knee length dress in pale blue. To one side, Lee and Cheryl sat playing with their son, Danny, Lee looking out of place in his dark blue suit, Cheryl perfectly at home in a dark, flowery dress, while Danny revelled in his smart, new short trousers, white shirt and bowtie.

Sheila and Brenda were checking their watches nervously when Joe stepped out of the lift.

"Pushing our luck," Brenda grumbled. "It's quarter to eleven. The bride will be here soon."

Joe had noticed her mood deteriorating on the drive over from Sanford.

"Yeah, well, it can't be happening too far away, can it? Gimme a minute." Ambling out of the bar, he approached the counter where Harriet Atkinson was busy with the computer. He rapped on the laminate top. "Excuse me?"

She peered at him over her glasses. "Yes?"

Joe swept his hands down from the shoulder. "Is this acceptable."

"Perfectly."

"Good. Only I'd hate to go into this wedding without passing your inspection first."

"Mr Murray—"

"Where is the wedding?"

Mrs Atkinson pointed along the entrance hall to a set of double doors where two burly ushers stood in attendance. "In the Beatrix Potter Room. Reception is in a marquee on the lawns. You're not the groom, are you?"

Joe frowned. "No."

"Thank heaven for that. Another poor girl saved."

21

***

Joe, Sheila and Brenda had been seated towards the rear of the room less than five minutes before Kelly arrived, dressed in flowing white and looking suitably radiant, to Handel's *Arrival of the Queen of Sheba*.

The civil ceremony passed quickly enough, interrupted only once when someone's mobile phone tweeted to announce a text message, and at length the Superintendent Registrar pronounced them man and wife, and took them off to one side for the formal signing of the register.

"She looks beautiful," Brenda said while they waited for the formalities to be completed.

"Such a pretty girl," Sheila agreed, "and young Wes looks magnificent in his morning suit."

"He looks a damn sight tidier than he does in his boiler suit," Joe commented. "Why'd she get married in white, though? I mean, they've been living together for the last two years according to Alec."

"Why shouldn't she marry in white?" Brenda asked.

"I just told you. They've been living together for two years. Look, when we were young, a bride wearing white symbolised, er…" Joe's ears coloured. "Purity."

Sheila giggled. "Don't be so coy, Joe. You mean virginity."

His ears coloured further. "Well, I didn't wanna use that word."

"In Sanford, it meant most brides were liars," Brenda grumbled.

"It's old hat, Joe," Sheila promised him. "The white wedding is a fairly modern convention anyway, and the bride can choose whatever colour she wants. And if you want to get technical about it, the original colour for purity is blue, not white."

Joe shook his head. "Nah, that can't be right. Alison got married in blue, and she hadn't seen hide nor hair of her, er, purity for years before I met her."

The Beatrix Potter room, a large bar/dining area if Joe was any judge, had been perfectly laid out with a wedding in mind. Predominantly white, with garlands and floral displays here and there, a rich red carpet lined the route the bride took to join her groom, the same path they would take out onto the lawns. White chairs had been arranged either side of the carpet, their backs to the open French windows of the exit, facing a small dais where bride, groom, the chief bridesmaid and best man would stand for the vows. The area set aside for the signing of the register was screened off to the right of centre.

Although he had not had time to talk to any of them, Joe recognised Wes and Rott right away. Neither had changed much since their school and apprenticeship days. Rott had put weight on, as Alec had told Joe, but Wes appeared as muscular and fit now as he had when he and Lee had played for the Sanford Bulls.

Accompanied by Buddy Holly singing *True Love Ways*, Wes and Kelly marched slowly out of the Beatrix Potter Room, and the crowd of family and guests followed them out into the sunshine bathing the lawns of the The Lakeside Manor Hotel.

Joe, Sheila and Brenda emerged into the hot day, and slipped discreetly to one side while the main group gathered for the photographer. Taking out his Sony DSLR camera, Joe set the autofocus, and made his way via a circuitous route, to stand behind the official photographer, and take snaps of his own.

"I'm not bothered," he had said to his two companions, "but I know you two will give me earache if I don't take pictures."

He spotted the photographer giving him a mean glance, returned a thin, apologetic but reassuring smile, and continued snapping away. At length, he signalled to Sheila and Brenda to come away from the rear of the family group, and gathering them, and Lee, Cheryl and Danny off to one side, took pictures of them, too.

As the official photograph session reached its natural end, he noticed others taking out their cameras, and looking for the natural poses, and there was one man he had not noticed before.

Casually dressed in jeans and a pale blue windjammer, yet wearing a white shirt and dark tie, broad shouldered and muscular, Joe guessed his age at about thirty. Sandy haired, serious looking, he took pictures in rapid succession on a Canon 650, which looked similar to Joe's Sony. But where Joe carried his two lenses in the pocket of his gilet (or in this case, his jacket) this man had a photographer's bag slung over his shoulder.

"I didn't notice him at the ceremony," Sheila commented when Joe pointed him out.

"And dressed like that, Attila would probably give him fifty lashes," Joe said. "Wonder who he is."

"Local press?" Brenda suggested. "They often poke their noses in at do's like this."

"Yeah right. Local plumber gets married. Story of the week, innit?"

At length, the party made their way to the marquee, where Joe and his companions found themselves sat on the outer periphery, while Lee, Cheryl and their son, were placed closer to the wedding party, as befitted close friends but not quite family.

Caterers had been brought in to handle the reception. Supervised by a tall, broad shouldered man in his early forties, his florid complexion matched by his bulging abdomen, they carried out their duties quickly and efficiently, and silently, Joe congratulated them. Catering for such events was an attractive proposition, but Joe had always been dissuaded by the time factor and the need to marshal the troops so perfectly.

There was one exception: a young man who looked

remarkably like the supervisor, but spent an undue length of time talking and joking with Rott and the chief bridesmaid, Darlene Garbutt.

"If he worked for me, he'd be on washing up detail," Joe commented.

"It would make a change from me," Brenda grumbled.

Joe was about to pick her up when their waiter arrived.

During the first course, for which Joe chose melon, Rott stood up and proposed a toast to the bride and groom, after which everyone settled down to a lunch of pan glazed chicken breast, followed by a choice of desserts, and plenty of fine wines.

By the time they came to the speeches, and Rott stumbled through his ten minute address, the long hours, good food and alcohol were beginning to take their toll on Joe, and when Wes and Kelly took to the floor for the first waltz, he almost nodded off. Only a nudge from Brenda prevented him.

"I've been up since five, you know," he complained.

With the formal part of the afternoon over, the party atmosphere began to kick in. Couples danced, others sat back and drank, Joe became more and more tired, and out front, Lee, Wes and Rott sat together, catching up on old times. Joe danced with Sheila and Brenda in turn, but it was at their insistence, and his lack of enthusiasm did not go unnoticed.

"Tonight, I'll be different," he assured them. "Cos when this is over, I'm going for a couple of hours' kip."

Ordering drinks at the makeshift bar, Joe found himself served by the catering supervisor.

"Bernard Vetch," he introduced himself. "I run the Waterside Inn."

Joe was puzzled. "You've shut down you pub to run this gig?"

"Have I hell as like shut down the pub," Vetch replied. "I'm a businessman, not a bloody muppet. I got a crew in to man the pub while I supervised this lot here." He waved along the bar. "Trust me, in catering you can't leave anything to your staff. You have to do it yourself."

"Tell me about it. I run a trucker's café in Sanford." Handing over his money, Joe nodded along the bar at the younger version of Vetch. "You should be having a word with yon fella. He spent far too long chatting up the bridesmaid."

Vetch scowled. "He's my son, Carl. And he knows Darlene quite well."

Joe remained unimpressed. "All the more reason for screaming at him." He pointed to Lee. "He's my nephew and he works for me, which means I kick his backside harder than anyone else's."

At one thirty, Lee, Rott, Wes and his bride came over to speak with Joe and his companions, and there followed a few minutes of animated conversation, while they reminisced on younger days when the three men all addressed Joe as Uncle Joe. Even now, they maintained a healthy respect, addressing them as Mr Murray, Mrs Riley and Mrs Jump.

Joe found Kelly a little reserved. A primary school teacher, when Sheila and Brenda tried to draw her into the conversation, all he could gather was that she was originally from Windermere, although she spoke with a near-perfect, classless accent, generated by three years at university and a year of teacher training.

She was what Joe would describe as beautiful in a classic way. Shapely, fine-boned, with flawless skin and complexion, he imagined that she took good care of herself, and if he tended to concentrate on her cleavage, he insisted it was because when she leaned forward to hear and speak to him, so much of it was on display.

His attention on her finer points did not go unnoticed, however, and when the young people left to do the rounds of other peripheral guests, both Sheila and Brenda chastised him for it.

"I wasn't staring," he insisted. "There wasn't anywhere else to look."

"Not staring?" Brenda scowled. "If your eyes had come any further out of their sockets, they'd have been hanging down on your cheeks."

By two o'clock, fatigue was taking an even bigger toll on him. He wandered through the seats and around the edge of the dance floor to the high table, where he leaned over to speak with Alec and Julia Staines.

"A good do," he congratulated them, "but I'm feeling the strain. I need some sleep, so I'm gonna shoot off back to my room. I'll see you tonight."

"The disco is in here, Joe, not the hotel." Julia told him. "Officially starts at eight o'clock, but they'll be serving drinks a good hour before that." She smiled fondly. "And you pick up your own bill."

Joe gave her a lopsided grin. "You bloody Yorkshire folk. Never did learn how to spend money, did you?"

Alec was about to riposte, but a commotion near the marquee entrance caught his attention. "What the hell's going on?"

Joe turned to watch.

At the entrance, the photographer he had seen earlier was haranguing Darlene, the chief bridesmaid. Rott and Carl Vetch had come to Darlene's aid and voices were raised. They could not hear what was being said over the music, but it was clear that Rott was on the verge of losing his temper. Lee and Wes were holding him back, but he continued to point, shout and wave threatening fists at the intruder.

Eventually the two ushers, both similar in size and build to Wes, Lee and Rott, grabbed the photographer and marched him away, Wes and Lee persuaded Rott to sit down, and Carl Vetch comforted a distraught Darlene..

Joe crossed the floor to the entrance, where he was joined by Sheila and Brenda, and they watched the ushers escort the interloper out.

"Where were you when things needed calming down?" Sheila asked.

"Talking to Alec and Julia. Besides, it looked to me like Wes and Lee did a good enough job on Rott." He watched as the two ushers began to push the photographer more forcefully, and then one threw a punch. That was enough for Joe. "Excuse me," he said to the women, and walked briskly out onto the lawns, hurrying to the putative fight. "Hey," he called out. "You two. That's enough. Let him be."

The usher turned to scowl at him, and he saw for the first time that they were brothers.

"He's been hassling Darlene," said one.

"You mean she's been hassling me," the photographer complained, only to stare at another raised, threatening fist.

"Knock it off," Joe demanded.

"Just push off, granddad, and mind your own business."

"Don't talk to my Uncle Joe like that."

Surprised by the intervention, Joe half turned to find Lee behind him. The ushers stood back a little.

Concentrating on the pair, Joe said, "See? Don't speak to me like that." He jerked a thumb at the shaken photographer. "I think he's got the message, so leave him alone." He turned on the photographer. "And you, use your nut. I don't know what your beef is—"

"I—"

"And I don't wanna know," Joe cut him off. "But this isn't the time, or the place to bring it up. Now bugger off while you're still in one piece."

The photographer glowered. "You tell her, it doesn't end here. I will be back."

One of the ushers took a pace forward, and the photographer beat a hasty retreat.

Joe watched him leave and eyed the two ushers, now making their way back to the marquee.

"What was it all about, Lee?" he asked as they began to

retrace their steps.

"Dunno, Uncle Joe. That bloke were giving Darlene some verbal and Rott fancies her, so he poked his oar in. Me and Wes had to hold him back, then Aunty Sheila sent me after you when she saw them two threatening you."

"Good of her."

"She were bothered for you, Uncle Joe, and you were right anyroad. They shouldn't have been knuckling him."

"Good bouncers don't lose their temper," Joe agreed as they stepped out of the sunlight again.

"Oh, they're not just bouncers, Uncle Joe. They're Darlene's brothers, an'all."

# Chapter Three

When Joe woke, just after five thirty, and looked out through the windows, across the lawns of the hotel, little had changed other than the marquee appeared to be inhabited by fewer guests. Instead, smartly attired hotel porters and cleaners had taken over, obviously cleaning up and restocking the place for the evening disco.

Looking beyond the Lakeside's boundaries, to Lake Windermere itself, the crowds at the boat station had increased, along with traffic on the water. Thousands of people, he reflected, making an early start to what promised to be a hot and busy summer's weekend. On the far shore, he could make out tiny figures, hikers, he guessed, wandering the hills and valleys. He had never been able to understand the attraction.

"Gimme four wheels and an engine," he muttered, and came away from the window.

He had noticed some of the Lakeside guests lounging around in shorts and T-shirts, and with defiance built into him, he changed into his and prepared to outface Harriet Atkinson on reception.

He was not disappointed.

"The problem is not the shorts and T-shirt, Mr Murray," she said tartly, "but *your* shorts and T-shirt."

Taking affront, he demanded, "So what's wrong with them?"

Mrs Atkinson looked him up and down with distaste. His shorts were crumpled and at one time had been khaki, but were now a shade of dirty off-white. His dark blue and red, striped T-shirt was covered in various stains and cigarette ash, and at foot level, his trainers, the same ones he used while working in the Lazy Luncheonette, were almost hanging off his feet.

"Other guests wear smart sportswear. You're only short of a hard hat and you could be dressed for a day's work on a Spanish building site."

"Well, at least I could teach the bricklayers how to cook a proper steak. Now are you gonna stop me from enjoying a little sun on the lawns?"

She gave him another withering glance. "Unfortunately, I'm not permitted to do that, but I will report the matter to Mr Nelson."

"Well if he wants to see me, you know where he can find me. But warn him, if he hassles me, he'll end up with more than an eye and arm missing."

He made his way through the Beatrix Potter room, and out to the lawns. Looking around, he recognised most of the faces from the wedding and reasoned that Wes and Kelly must have taken over the whole place, at least for the day. Some people were sprawled on the grass, sleeping off the heat, others were on loungers. One or two people were making their way away from or towards the hotel along the narrow path which led to the church, and Joe guessed there must be an entrance hidden by the copse. Waiters scurried here and there, delivering tea or cold drinks. Most of the tables and loungers were taken, but he found an empty space towards the far end of the building, where he could bask in the afternoon sun, settled in and rolled a cigarette.

"It'd be nice if you could do this all the time, wouldn't it?"

Joe half turned to find Wes Staines standing behind him. He had changed out of his morning suit, but still wore a smart pair of casual trousers and white shirt, open at the neck.

"Hello, lad. Not with your new wife? Had enough of

married life already?" He patted the chair along side, inviting Wes to sit.

"She's sleeping it off, Mr Murray. Long day, and we have to get through the evening, too. Then we have to be up for about three tomorrow morning."

"Your dad was telling me. Maldives, isn't it? At least you'll still have sunny weather next week. According to form, we're losing it to rain by Monday."

Wes nodded. "Did you go anywhere exotic for your honeymoon?"

Lighting his cigarette, Joe grunted, a half laugh. "Exotic? Lloret-de-Mar. Costa Brava. Bit of a dump, if you want my opinion. And Alison took ill half way through the week. I spent the other half in the hotel bar, on my own."

Wes, too, lit a smoke, and glanced over Joe's attire. "How did you get past the Gestapo officer in reception dressed like that?"

"Sheer bottle. I'm too old to be intimidated by the likes of her, and if she thinks she has the franchise on plain speaking, she can think again." He abruptly changed the subject. "I was just thinking, Wes, I had no trouble getting rooms here, but most of these people," he waved around the fine lawns, "were at the wedding. Did you book the whole place, or something?"

He smiled shyly. "We *reserved* the entire hotel. It only has about forty rooms. Dad said you'd want to be near, so I asked them to keep three rooms back for you, your Lee and his missus and kid, and Mrs Riley and Mrs Jump. I mean, you coulda stayed somewhere cheaper if you'd wanted. I wouldn't have been offended."

"Money's no problem, Wes, and your dad did right. We're here for the weekend, and we do prefer quality accommodation. The days of seaside bed and breakfasts are history for us." He changed the subject again. "How's Rott? Has he calmed down yet?"

"Smashed out of his brains when he left with Darlene."

"Sounds as if his luck's in, though." Joe chuckled. "Traditional, innit? Best man scores with the chief bridesmaid."

Wes, too, laughed. "The state he's in, he'd never manage it. He's had a bit of a thing with her for a while now. Nowt serious, mind."

Joe drew on his cigarette and let the humour settle. "So who is she, this Darlene. Good friend of Kelly's, is she?"

"Best friend apparently," Wes replied. "They were in college together. You know. Teacher training. According to what Kelly told me, Darlene never made it, and they lost touch for a bit after Kelly moved up here. Then Darlene came to visit last year, and now she lives up here. Works in the big supermarket in Windermere. Checkout operator. Waste of an education, that."

"There's no shame in it, Wes. Someone has to man the checkouts, and I'm sure there'll be a valid reason for the girl not making it through teacher training."

"Men," Wes said.

To Joe it spoke of the huge gap between his and Wes's generation. When he was the lad's age, it would have been a damning indictment of the woman, but to modern youth it was nothing. Just another factor.

"Was that what that business was with that photographer bloke?"

"Pitman?"

"Is that his name."

Wes nodded. "Adam Pitman. I dunno what it's about, Mr Murray. Kelly was saying as how Darlene knew Pitman from London and he's been hassling her."

"Stalking her, or something?"

"Summat like that."

"Yeah, well, according to Pitman, it's the other way round. She's been giving him grief."

"Dunno," Wes repeated. "Musta been a while ago, though.

Like I say, Darlene has lived up here for over a year." He laughed. "Picked a wrong un there, mind. Rott's still a snapper, as you saw. If me and your Lee hadn't intervened, he'd have ripped Pitman's head off. And those brothers of hers, Jezza and Ricky. Not blokes you'd wanna hassle with."

"So I noticed." Joe took another pull on his cigarette and changed the subject again. "And what about you? Alec was saying business is good."

"Nonstop," Wes agreed. "I'm the plumber and gas man, Rott is the electrician, and we just have too much work." He lapsed into a thoughtful silence for a moment. "Me dad is like you, you know. When me and your Lee were playing for the Sanford Bulls, Dad insisted I went to night school and learned a trade, just like you did with Lee. Cos you couldn't rely on making a good, steady living playing rugby. And he were right, Mr Murray. Your Lee got his knee busted up and the coach stopped picking me after a few bad games, and I'm better off dealing with water heaters, lavatories and gas fires."

"It's the wisdom of age, Wes. When your dad and I left school, we didn't have a choice." Joe laughed cynically. "If I'd had the option, I'd have been a copper, but even if I'd been tall enough, my old dad wouldn't have let it happen."

"Bit of a come down for Kelly, though. A teacher marrying a plumber."

"Gar, don't talk rubbish." Joe watched Wes stub out his cigarette. "She obviously doesn't think so, or she wouldn't have married you. Never be ashamed of what you do for a living, Wes. Skilled lads like you are just as important to the world as intelligent women like your missus. Besides, you're not just a plumber, you're businessman, too. That's the way I look at it when people try to belittle me for running a truckers' caff."

"S'pose you're right." Wes yawned. "I'd better go see how Her Indoors is. Nice talking to you, Mr Murray."

"And you, Wes. And by the way, you're a big boy, now. You can call me Joe."

"If I did, me mother would have a fit. See you later." Wes picked up his cigarettes and lighter and walked off, leaving Joe to bask in the hot, afternoon sunshine.

Within a few minutes a pair of familiar figures appeared on the path behind the clump of trees, and trudged wearily up the hill. Still dressed in their wedding finery, Joe would have recognised Sheila and Brenda in the crowd at a football match, but he was puzzled as to how they had acquired carrier bags.

He flagged down a passing waiter. "Bring me three teas, son, and some cakes."

The lad nodded and carried on into the building.

Soon, Sheila and Brenda joined him. They were sweating, flushed and exhausted.

Joe grinned at Brenda. "Have you been teaching Sheila some lessons in the bushes?"

Sheila flopped onto the chair alongside him, Brenda the other side. She held up several carrier bags bearing famous High Street names. "We've been shopping." Although her reply was innocuous enough, Joe noticed it did not match her angry features.

Joe's smile turned to a frown. "I didn't know the The Lakeside Manor had a branch of Boots or WH Smiths, and why did they hide it behind those bushes?"

"We caught the bus to Windermere," Sheila explained. "Dear me, it's hot."

"Hot enough to fry eggs on the pavement," Brenda agreed sulkily.

"It's the heat that does it," Joe said as the waiter returned. "Stick it on the room, will you, son? Room eleven." While the waiter went away, he poured tea for the two women and pushed the cake plate to them. "Do you mean there's a way out down the hill and behind the bushes? Not very secure is it? I mean anyone could wander in and camp out on the lawn to take the sun for an hour."

"There's a gate," Sheila explained gulping down a much

needed mouthful of tea. "You use your room key to work it."

"Ah. I see." The system became clear in Joe's mind. Like so many hotels, the Lakeside Manor used electronic room keys similar in size to a credit card. "So did you spend much in Windermere?"

"We'll need a pay rise to cover it," Sheila told him, chewing on an individual bakewell tart.

"Looks like you're going to be in debt for a while, then."

"How about you, Joe. Have you had a good afternoon?"

He stirred sugar into his tea. "I've had a good rest, if that's what you mean, and I'm fit for the fray tonight."

"Tomorrow we thought we might take a boat ride on the lake, and visit Beatrix Potter's farm over at Sawrey," Brenda said. "You have to cross the lake and then it's a few miles by bus."

"We're sure Danny would love it," Sheila said.

"Bit old for Beatrix Potter, isn't he?" Joe asked. "But, yeah, whatever you want. Not too early, though."

Brenda scowled. "Are you on a promise, Joe Murray?"

"Depends. Are you promising?"

"Bugger off."

Still wondering what he had done to incur Brenda's displeasure, Joe said, "By my reckoning we'll all need a good night's sleep tonight."

Sheila yawned. "I don't know about tonight, I need a nod right now. The minute I've finished this tea."

\*\*\*

Wearing a pair of casual trousers and equally casual, short sleeved shirt beneath his ubiquitous gilet, Joe met Sheila and Brenda in reception just before eight o'clock, and accompanied them across the lawns to the marquee where guests were already buying in their first drinks.

The seating had been changed to accommodate more

dancers, the tables now arranged in narrower groups around the inner perimeter of the marquee. Joe secured them seating near one of the three exits.

"Easier for me to sneak out for a smoke," he explained.

He need not have worried. Sheila and Brenda were not disposed to argue. The day had been one of searing heat; even with the sun setting, there was hardly a breath of wind to cool them off.

"Sitting near the exit may be just a fraction of a degree cooler," Sheila told him.

The DJ set the party in motion at bang on eight o'clock with Bill Haley and the Comets and *Rock Around The Clock*, and Joe, invigorated after his peaceful afternoon was one of the first on the floor with Sheila, much to the amusement and admiration of the other guests.

Their performance encouraged others to join in and by the time the bride and groom arrived, a few minutes later, the bar was packed and the dance floor crowded.

Twenty minutes later, the disco was in full swing, the party mood catching everyone. The bride and groom were jiggling around the floor, matched by Rott and Darlene; Lee and Cheryl were close by, Sheila and Brenda making up another pair along with Alec and Julia Staines. Joe had been out for a smoke and was sitting it out with his great nephew, Danny, keeping the boy entertained, showing him how to fold paper serviettes into different, often unidentifiable, shapes.

"It's a swan," Joe protested when Danny asked what the latest figure was supposed to be.

"It doesn't look like a swan, Uncle Joe," Danny observed. "Swans have long necks."

"All right, so it's a duck."

"But ducks don't have all them feathers."

Joe tutted. "Giving you a computer for Christmas was a bad move, wasn't it?"

Danny declared his undying love for the computer, but Joe

was not listening. Two women had entered the marquee on the far side, and were making their way through the sea of tables and chairs towards he DJ's dais.

"If they're guests, I'll eat my new cap," Joe muttered.

They had about them that air of officialdom here on business, and not simply extended family coming to offer their best wishes to the newlyweds. The shorter of the pair, clad in a dark blouse and trousers, carrying large handbag, kept talking over her shoulder to her partner, a blonde, younger, slightly taller but dressed in the same, simple manner.

Joe watched their steady progress until they stood alongside the DJ and spoke directly to him. He saw the older woman pull out a wallet and show it to the DJ, who argued momentarily. She pointed to the set, and he faded the music.

Picking up the microphone, the elder woman came to the front of the makeshift stage.

"Ladies and gentlemen, forgive me for interrupting your evening." Her voice boomed around the tent. "I am Detective Inspector Geraldine Perry, Cumbria Police, and this is Detective Constable Fiona Lesney. Is Mr Paul Drummond here, please?"

Rott stepped forward and the two women stepped off the stage to meet him.

"You stay here like a good boy, Danny," Joe ordered. "Your mum and dad will be back in a minute." Joe hurried across the floor, weaving his way through the stalled dancers, nudging Lee and ordering him back to the table to look after Danny. Squeezing through to the front, he ranged himself alongside Alec Staines and Wes.

Addressing Rott, Perry asked, "Do you know a man named Adam Pitman?"

Rott shrugged. "Never heard of him."

"I see. Our information is that you had an altercation with him earlier today. He's a photographer."

"Oh him. Yeah, we've met. What about him? Reported me

for threatening him, has he?"

"I'll have to ask you to come with us to the station, Mr Drummond."

"Why? I'm at a bloody wedding. I'm best man, for God's sake."

"We need to question you on certain, er, matters regarding Mr Pitman."

Joe edged forward into the open space between the dancers and the police. "Hold on, Rott. Before you go, you have a right to know exactly what they're going to question you on."

Rott smiled at the two police officers. "See. Now why?"

"This gentleman is your lawyer, is he?"

Rott would have answered, but Joe got there first. "It doesn't matter who I am. I know his rights. This is a wedding party, for God's sake. You can't just march in here and haul him away without at least telling him what it's in aid of."

"Yes, well, sir, it's because this is a wedding party that I had hoped to avoid the announcement, but if you're going to push me…" Perry trailed off.

"What is Rott… I mean Paul, supposed to have done?"

Perry rounded on Rott and with great formality, announced. "Mr Drummond, I must ask you to accompany us back to the station where you will be questioned on suspicion of the murder of Adam Pitman."

# Chapter Four

The stunned silence which greeted Perry's announcement quickly broke down into a babble of muttered conversation and loud protests from Wes and his bride.

"I had nowt to do with it," Rott shouted above the hubbub.

"You must come to the station and give us a formal statement," the inspector told him. "If you refuse, I shall call for backup and arrest you. And trust me, Mr Drummond, I don't care how big you are, there are plenty of officers in Windermere who can bring you in."

"I didn't do nothing," Rott shouted again.

"Go with them, son," Joe intervened. "If you don't, you only make matters worse. Go to the station, give them the statement. There'll be plenty of beer and grub left when you get back." He scribbled his mobile number on a piece of paper. "If you have any serious problems, bell me and I'll help clear your name, but for now, go with them."

Perry stared at him again, the malevolence quite clear in her brown eyes. "Are you a lawyer, sir?"

"No. I'm Joe Murray. That probably means nothing to you." He transferred his attention to the detective constable. "You. Chesney—"

"Lesney," she corrected.

"Whoever. Get onto Detective Sergeant Gemma Craddock, West Yorkshire Police. She's based in Sanford. Ask about her Uncle Joe." He swung back to Perry. "When you've spoken to Rott and then spoken to our Gemma, you'll know where to find me."

Wes Staines stepped forward. "Just a minute. This Pitman bloke was seen off this afternoon. He never turned up here again, and we know for a fact that Rott was in his room all day."

"In that case, there won't be any problem, will there."

"And what about these kids?" Joe asked, jerking a thumb sideways at Wes. "They're just married, and they're going on honeymoon in the early hours. You gonna hold 'em back?"

Perry sighed. "At the moment, Mr Murray, I have no need to speak to Mr Staines. Depending on the outcome of our interview with Mr Drummond, I may need to, but if that's so, I'll come back later this evening so as to give them a chance to get away. Is that all right with you?"

"You're knocking on the wrong doors," Joe insisted and walked away.

While some of the crowd hassled the police officers, Sheila and Brenda hurried after Joe.

"What are you doing?" Brenda demanded. "You can't leave it like this."

"I don't have any choice," he responded. "They're taking Rott in, they may hold Wes and Kelly back. All I can do is make some inquiries while they're talking to the lad. See if we can't clear their names indirectly." He carried on walking out of the marquee, where he rolled a cigarette.

"So what are you going to do, Joe?" Sheila asked.

His engraved, brass Zippo flared in the fading daylight. Taking a deep drag on the cigarette, he coughed violently, and struggled to bring his breathing under control. As the fit settled, he gazed across the lawns towards the lake, where the midsummer sun had already dropped behind the hills on the far shore, leaving a glorious, crimson sky in its wake. He looked back at the hotel, and finally he swung his gaze round to the car park, where the lights were already in evening shadow, but had not yet come on.

"We know that Rott was in his room. According to young

Wes, he'd scored with the bridesmaid."

"Really, Joe," Sheila disapproved. "Must you be so… so vulgar?"

"The kid is being questioned on murder, Sheila. I don't have time for linguistic niceties. He was with the bridesmaid. She should be able to clear his name, but let's assume she was as drunk as him, and she can't. If he killed this bod, he must have left not only the room, but the hotel."

"How do you know?" Brenda asked.

Joe waved at the lawns. "Look around. You see any cops here? No. This Pitman bloke wasn't killed here or we'd be swarming in SOCOs. He was murdered somewhere out there." Now he waved vaguely towards the lake. "To do that, Rott must have left the hotel altogether."

"Logical enough," Sheila said. "What's your point? Someone may have seen him?"

"Someone or something. You enjoy the party – if you can – I'll go and have a word with the vicious old bat on reception."

"That attitude is not going to get you very far, Joe," Sheila admonished him.

"All right, so I'll be diplomatic. I'll drop the 'vicious'. Catch you in a bit."

He strode off across the lawns and emerged onto the car park at the corner of the hotel. Looking up at the tall lighting post, he spotted CCTV cameras surrounding the cluster of lamps.

Killing time to finish his cigarette, he let his agile mind create different scenarios. He gazed along the road, to where it crested a small rise, and then dropped out of sight. He checked the bushes and hedgerows lining the road, then spun to look back over the lawns, past the wedding marquee and the path that led to the lakeside road.

Taking a final drag, dropping the cigarette on the ground and crushing it underfoot, he strode along, past the ivy covered walls of the hotel front, and entered through the main doors to find a tall, slender, immaculately attired, officious-looking man on duty behind the counter.

"Where's Boadicea?"

Identified by his name tag as *Thomas Nelson, General Manager*, he cast a suspicious glance over the rim of his spectacles. "I beg your pardon, sir?"

"You know. Attila the Hen. The frump you had on duty earlier."

"You mean Mrs Atkinson? She's off duty. Can I be of assistance?" Nelson's tones were distinctly imperious, giving the impression that the last thing he wanted was to be of assistance.

Joe tutted. "I suppose you'll have to do. I'm Joe Murray, and—"

"Ah, yes. Mr Murray. I have a note here about your attitude and appearance." He searched around the counter, rifling through a small stack of papers. "I have to tell you, Mr Murray, that The Lakeside Manor Hotel does not—"

"Just shut up," Joe interrupted. "Stop waffling and tell me what kind of CCTV coverage do you have outside the building?"

The question caused another frown. "This is a discreet hotel, sir. We have very important people staying here at odd times during the year. Politicians, business leaders, even minor royalty. It's why we insist our guests be suitably attired at all times, and we do not give out any kind of information on our security measures."

Joe struggled to control his irritation. "Listen, sunbeam, the cops have just turned up and hauled off one of the wedding guests on suspicion of murder."

The supercilious front broke. Nelson's mouth fell open, his eyes opened wide in a mask of pure horror. "Murder... but... but... The Lakeside Manor doesn't accommodate murderers."

Joe's anger began to get the better of him "How would you know? You never asked me if I was a killer when I rang to book, and according to your chief henchwoman, your brochure stipulates correct dress at all times, but I never noticed it saying, 'By the way, if you're a murderer don't bother booking'."

Nelson shook his head. "No, no. That's not what I meant. I was thinking of our reputation."

"A man's been murdered, you idiot. No one cares about your reputation. Now tell me about your security cameras."

The manager appeared to be calming down. "You're a police officer are you?"

"No. I'm a… a private investigator, but I have contact with the cops. Now, for the last time, tell me what kind of coverage you have on CCTV?"

Nelson cleared his throat. "Let's see now, we have the car park and main entrance covered, naturally… and that's about it."

Joe stared. "You don't have the gate down across the lawns covered?"

Nelson shook his head. "No need. The gate is secure. It can only be opened by one of our room keys. Mr Murray, are you suggesting the killer sneaked into these grounds?"

The flicker of hope in his voice did not escape Joe's attention. He was quick to extinguish it. "No. The police are saying he sneaked out of here."

***

Inspector Perry led Constable Lesney into the cramped room normally occupied by the duty officer, and waved her to a seat. "You spoke to Sergeant Craddock, Fiona?"

"Yes, guv. She took a bit of tracking down. Out on the tiles, but I found her and we had a good natter."

Perry took her seat behind the desk, Lesney sat opposite. "So what did she have to say about our Mr Murray?"

"Close friend of the groom's father. He's also one hell of a part time detective."

Perry's eyebrows rose. "Is he, indeed?"

Lesney nodded. "Do you remember the Valentine Strangler. Busy man in West Yorkshire until he was nicked earlier this year."

"I recall reading of it, yes."

"Murray was a suspect. Not a serious one, but he was interviewed under caution. He ripped the local force to bits when he turned up the real killer. In Weston-super-Mare over Easter, he managed to pin down a pair of triple murderers. A double killing at New Year in Lincoln, and the killer of an MP in York last year. He's an astute man and according to Sergeant Craddock, while he may be a pain in the backside, it's not wise to cross him because he won't back off and he'll make you look completely incompetent."

"Assuming we don't already have the killer locked up."

Anticipation lit Lesney's face. "He's confessed?"

"No, Fiona, he hasn't. He says he never left the hotel all afternoon. In fact, he insists he was asleep at the time of the killing, and we're going to have a hard time proving otherwise unless we can find the murder weapon, or some other indication that he was there. He did, however, give me information which may put us on another track." Perry checked her watch and stood up. "Almost ten o'clock. The difficult bit will be telling the bride and groom that they can't go on their honeymoon tomorrow. Come on."

\*\*\*

Joe sat grim and silent, his gaze intent upon the bride and groom as Kelly burst into tears and Wes struggled to console her. Nearby, Alec and Julia Staines, and Kelly's parents harangued Inspector Perry, whose stern features remained impassive and immovable. Sheila and Brenda were on hand to offer sympathy to the young couple, while the bridesmaid,

45

Darlene and her two brothers stood awkwardly to one side in a small group composed of themselves, Lee, Cheryl and Danny, and other guests.

Perry detached herself from the argument, leaving her constable to deal with the angry parents and distressed couple. She strode purposefully across the dance floor, under the venomous gaze of many eyes, making straight for him.

He, too, was angry; angry with the police, angry with the idiot – whoever he or she was – who had done so much to ruin this special day for the couple. But as Perry neared him, he buried the anger, and instead maintained the same passivity that he saw in the inspector's face.

"Mr Murray—"

"Fine start to married life for them isn't it?"

Perry was nonplussed by his interruption. "I beg your pardon?"

Joe waved a hand at the scene around them. "You know, I've never been any good at this game. Relationships, marriage and stuff. I envy those who can do it. People like Alec and Julia, my nephew, Lee and his wife Cheryl, and even my friends, Brenda and Sheila. But I don't envy Wes and Kelly. This is one wedding they'll never forget. Interrupted by a murder, best man questioned, and now you've just told them they can forget the honeymoon."

Perry sat opposite him, her back to the angry guests. "And how would you know that?"

"I watch what's going on around me." Joe pointed to each eye in turn. "Nothing much gets past these. You turn up, the bride's in tears, it's not likely to be for Rott, is it? He's only a friend and that would be something to worry about, not break down over."

"Hmm. Your niece said you were smart and direct."

"You spoke to her then?"

"My constable did. Mr Murray, this is a murder investigation, and according to your niece, Sergeant Craddock, you, more than anyone, should appreciate what that means. After speaking to Mr Drummond, I now have cause to restrict the movements of Wesley and Kelly Staines, and Darlene Garbutt. I'm sorry, but if we were to allow them to leave the area, never mind the country, it would be a dereliction of duty."

Joe nodded. "You smoke?"

"No."

"I do. Let's step out while I enjoy a fix." He stood, walked out of the marquee, and began to roll a cigarette.

With the time coming up to 10.30pm, night had come, and the brighter stars shone in sky, but behind the hills on the other side of the lake, the faint glow of twilight could still be seen. Closer to them, the boat station was alive with coloured lights, and when Joe concentrated his eyes, he could make out crowds of people still enjoying the warm evening.

His Zippo flared, illuminating his features as he lit the cigarette. Blowing out a satisfied stream of smoke, then breaking down into a coughing fit, he regained control of his breathing and demanded, "Gimme the bottom line."

"Sergeant Craddock said you would insist," Perry replied. "And I don't object, but I want to make one or two things clear. This is a particularly violent and nasty crime."

"Murder usually is."

"I know, but this is worse than normal. There's no point in my telling you to mind your own business, because I know you won't. If, however, you should come across anything, anything at all, you bring it to me. You do not pursue this alone. Agreed?"

"Yeah, yeah. I get the picture. Now what happened?"

"There was an altercation here today, about three o'clock, involving Darlene Garbutt and Adam Pitman."

Joe drew on his cigarette. "I know. I saw it. Darlene's brothers threw him out."

"So we understand, but Paul Drummond was the main

protagonist. He was heard to threaten Pitman. At seven thirty, we received a call to an old, disused boathouse just along the waterfront from the boat station." Perry waved a flaccid hand towards the lake. "Adam Pitman was found hanging by his camera strap in that old shed. When his body was taken down, the doctor found a large wound on his head. He had been hit by something heavy. Very heavy. Practically caved his head in. Nearby, we also found a pair of overalls. We're testing them for the usual traces, but we believe they belong to Paul Drummond."

Taking another pull on the cigarette, Joe argued, "Rott was blasted out of his brains this afternoon. If he hit Pitman, it would have been more by luck than judgement that he caught him the right blow to kill him, and he was in no condition to lift him up and hang him."

"Drummond says the same, but we're moving cautiously. In the meantime, he tells us that Staines the younger and his wife also knew Pitman, and Wes Staines may have had cause to kill him. Now do you understand why I can't let them fly off to the Maldives?"

Joe ruminated a moment on the details, took another drag on his cigarette, and asked, "What was the problem between Darlene and Pitman?"

"Drummond isn't sure. He, apparently, has some kind of relationship with Darlene, but it's casual, so he doesn't know her that well, and what he's told us is what she told him."

"And that is?"

"Pitman has been stalking Darlene."

"Pitman claimed it was the other way round."

Perry was surprised. "Did he now?"

Joe nodded, took a final drag on his cigarette, and as he stubbed it out, suffered another violent coughing fit. Struggling to breathe properly for a moment, he took out his tobacco tin and began to roll another.

"You can hardly catch your breath, yet you want another

cigarette?" Perry observed.

He shook his head. "Not want, need. It's the hot weather. Affects my breathing. Some… sometimes, taking a drag is enough to make me cough up whatever crap is in the way." Joe lit the fresh smoke, pulled on it, and went through another racking cough before heaving in his breath. Tears of exertion sparkling in his eyes, he said, "That's better."

Perry shook her head sadly. "Smokers. I've never understood them. Now, Mr Murray—"

"Call me Joe. Please. I hate this formal stuff."

"Very well, Joe. You say Pitman claimed the argument was the other way round."

While his breathing came back under control, Joe gave her a brief rundown of events as he had seen them, and his exchange with the Garbutt brothers.

"The last thing he said was 'it doesn't end here', and he promised he would be back."

"In that case, I really need to speak to Darlene, get some background on this whole issue." Perry's attitude became friendlier, more conciliatory. "Listen, Joe, you can help. You know these people. They'll speak more freely to you than they will to me. I'm a cop: a symbol of authority, and that puts them on their guard. Whatever you learn, please come to me with it."

"Sure. No problem; one thing, though. Let's try and clear Wes and Kelly. Tonight. Give them the chance to get on that plane first thing in the morning."

She chewed her lip. "I don't know that it will be possible, but I'll do my best. Can you account for either of them today?"

Now it was Joe's turn to worry at his lip while he engaged his memory. "I can tell you where Wes was at about six o'clock. He was with me, over there." He pointed vaguely to the tables at the corner of the hotel. "We had a chat for a few minutes, then he said he was going to wake Kelly, get ready for

49

the evening disco."

"But you didn't follow him, so you don't know for sure."

"I can tell you that he didn't go down the path to the bottom gate." Again Joe pointed, this time down towards the main road and lakeside.

"You're sure?"

He nodded and dragged on his cigarette again. After another nasty bout of coughing, he said, "Less than a minute after he left, my two friends, Mrs Riley and Mrs Jump, came up from that gate. If Wes had gone that way, I'd have noticed, and they would have seen him. No. He went towards the car park, but he could have gone into the hotel through the Beatrix Potter Room."

"Equally, he could have gone to his car," Perry pointed out.

Joe nodded. "True. But the hotel has CCTV on the car park, so it won't be difficult to prove one way or the other."

"How much longer did you sit out there?"

"Ten, fifteen, twenty minutes. I don't know. I had a cup of tea with my friends, then they went back to their room to snatch a nap, and I went back to mine to shower and change for this evening." Joe weighed up the thin information at his disposal. "Do you have a time of death?"

"No. Pathologists. They're the worst." Perry gave a cynical little laugh. "When I got to the boathouse, about half past seven, the most the doctor would say was sometime between three and six thirty. So Wes Staines could have killed him before he sat out here with you."

"True, but there was no sign of blood on him."

"Did he join you, or was it the other way round?"

Silently, Joe congratulated the inspector. It was a question he would have got around to eventually. That she made it before him spoke of a meticulous investigator. "He joined me, and no, I didn't see which direction he came from, other than, again, it wasn't up the path from the lake. He must have come from the hotel, but whether we're talking car park or from the inside, I couldn't say."

"And what about Kelly?" Perry asked.

Joe shrugged. "I don't know. I only have Wes's say that she was in their room."

"We'd better speak to them."

They turned to go back into the marquee. As they did, a furious Julia Staines met them.

"Joe Murray, what the hell is going on?"

"Take it easy, Julia—"

"Why are you letting this... this bloody woman stop my son going away on his honeymoon?"

"It's nothing to do with—"

Perry cut him off. "Mrs Staines, I'm trying, right now, to clear your son and his wife from this investigation, so they can catch their flight."

"Do you seriously imagine Wes or Kelly had anything to do with this?" Julia's anger was reaching boiling point. "You know him, Joe."

"I knew him," Joe replied. "I haven't seen him for years. Julia—"

"And you think he's changed so much he could do something like this?"

"Julia—"

Again she cut Joe off. "Shut it. Just don't speak to me, Joe Murray. Ever again."

She turned and stormed back into the marquee. Looking helplessly apologetic, Alec Staines gave an embarrassed half smile.

"Sorry, Joe. I know it's not your fault."

"It's okay, Alec. I think in her place, I'd be just as angry."

# Chapter Five

They made their way to one side of the dance floor where Constable Lesney was speaking with Darlene and her brothers.

"Could a woman have done this?" Joe asked.

"A woman could certainly have administered the blow that killed him," Perry replied. "Whether she could have lifted his body and hung him on the wall is a different matter. Pitman was quiet stocky, but that doesn't rule women out. Difficult but not impossible is the way I'm viewing it at the moment."

"Anything on his camera, or haven't you checked it yet?"

"There was no camera," Perry said. "Only the strap."

"What do you know about Pitman?" Joe asked as Sheila and Brenda made their determined way towards him.

"That is for the morning," the inspector replied. "All we know at the moment is he's a Londoner, and he's based in Dagenham. We don't know why he was here, what he was doing, unless, of course, he really was stalking Darlene, in which case, it makes absolute sense."

His two companions blocked his way.

"Joe, what the hell is going on?" Brenda demanded. "Julia is out of her mind, and she says it's your fault."

He shrugged. "What else is new? Someone would blame me for World War Two if I'd been born at the time."

Sheila was more moderate. "What's happening, Joe?"

"Wes and Kelly need to account for their whereabouts," he explained. "If they can do that, then Inspector Perry will allow them to catch their flight. If they can't, they'll have to claim on their insurance."

"This is outrageous," Brenda said.

"It is procedure, madam," Perry replied. "We're not talking a bit of shoplifting. A man has been murdered. I cannot let anyone leave unless and until they can satisfactorily account for their whereabouts between four o'clock and seven this afternoon, and that applies particularly to Mr and Mrs Staines."

"You know the score," Joe told his friends. "I don't think Wes or Kelly had anything to do with it, but until we know that for sure, they won't be allowed to leave. I'll tell you something else, too, it would help if people got off my back, and hers—" He indicated Inspector Perry, "— and let us get on with the job."

"You let them do this to your friends?" Brenda shouted. "You are impossible." She stormed off.

Joe shook his head. "I expect better of Brenda."

"I'm sorry, Joe," Sheila apologised. "She's really upset over this. It's the wedding thing. I'll talk to her."

He nodded, Sheila wandered off, and he and Perry continued on their way to join Lesney.

The constable took them off to one side, leaving Darlene and her brothers to twiddle their thumbs.

"Well, Fiona?" Perry asked.

Constable Lesney looked suspiciously at Joe.

"Whatever you have to say, you can say in front of Mr Murray," Perry encouraged.

"Pitman and Darlene Garbutt had a thing in London a year or two back. She was modelling for him. But he became possessive, and when she wanted out, he wouldn't accept it, so she moved up here to get away from him. Today was the first she'd seen of him since she left London a year ago, but she insists he has been hassling her by text message."

"So how did he know where to find her?" Joe asked.

Lesney shrugged. "She doesn't know, but it could be something to do with her brothers. They still live in London.

They're professional security officers with their own business."

"Muscle, you mean," Joe said, and again the constable shrugged. "I saw the way they dealt with Pitman this afternoon, and if they're professional security men, I'm a cordon bleu chef."

"And if they're so professional, what were they doing talking about their sister's location and this wedding?" Perry asked.

"Dunno, guv, but it might be that Pitman simply overheard them in a pub or something. Let's face it, once he got here, he wouldn't have any trouble pinning the wedding location down, would he?"

"According to Mr Murray, Pitman claimed that she was harassing him, not the other way round."

"Dunno, ma'am. I'm only telling you what she's just told me." Lesney consulted her notes. "Tell you what, though, she did say that Kelly, the bride, she was a model for Pitman, too."

"That squares with what Drummond told me," Perry said. "You carry on with Darlene and her brothers, Fiona. It's time I had a word with the bride and groom."

"You want me to back out?" Joe asked.

"No. In fact, I'd rather you sat with me. You know these people."

Lesney returned to her inquiries. Joe and Perry crossed the floor to the table beside the dais where Wes and Kelly were being comforted by friends and family.

"Mr Staines, Mrs Staines, we need to speak to you. In private," Perry announced.

Julia rounded viciously on her. "Leave them alone. Haven't you done enough damage?"

"Julia—" Alec began, only to be cut off by his furious wife.

"And you can shut up, too. If you had any balls, you wouldn't let her do this to them." She glowered at Joe. "And as for you—"

"Not interested," Joe interrupted.

They were seconds away from all-out war. Perry moved to

calm matters.

"Mrs Staines," she said to Julia, "I understand how you feel, how your son and his wife feel, but this is a murder investigation. Wesley and his wife will not get on that plane until I have spoken to them, in private. When I am satisfied, and only when I am satisfied that they had nothing to do with Mr Pitman's death, they will be free to enjoy their honeymoon."

"They had nothing to do with it," Julia screamed.

"The only way you could know that is if you did it," Perry retorted, "and quite frankly, looking at you, I doubt that you would have the strength."

Julia's fury erupted. She launched herself at Perry. Joe moved between them, and Julia's arm, her fist clenched, arcing round to strike the policewoman, caught him on the side of the head.

Joe tottered and sank to the floor, dazed and coughing. Alec and Wes moved to restrain Julia. Sheila bent to help Joe to his feet. Standing nearby, Brenda glared.

"Anymore of that," Perry warned, "and I will charge you with assault, Mrs Staines."

"It's all right," Joe insisted, and coughed harder. "She's just upset. I'm sure she didn't mean it."

Brenda glared harder. "She didn't hit you hard enough."

Joe rounded on her, coughing once more. "Brenda, if you've nothing constructive to add, bugger off to the bar and stoke up your alcohol levels."

Brenda walked away, and Sheila commiserated.

"Brenda's very upset, Joe. You know what she's like. She'll calm down."

"She can please her bloody self," Joe snapped, and coughed again. "She didn't object to me helping the cops when she was nailed for that killing in Chester, did she?"

"I'll speak to her. I promise. Now are you all right?"

He coughed again and his breathing began to settle. "I'm

fine. Deal with Brenda and Julia… if you can."

Sheila drifted off and with matters calmed, Wes spoke to Perry.

"What is it you want to know?"

"In private, Mr Staines."

Wes nodded, stood up and took Kelly's hand. "The hotel?"

Perry nodded, and led the way from the marquee, followed by Joe and the newlyweds.

The Beatrix Potter room had already been stripped of its temporary wedding décor, and returned to normal, the seating varicoloured in pastel shades of pink, yellow and green. The walls were adorned with pictures of Hilltop Farm and large framed reproductions of Jemima Puddleduck, Peter Rabbit, Squirrel Nutkin, and other, anthropomorphic characters from the author's work, including a large cartoon of Mr McGregor, whose florid, angry features reminded Joe of a caricature he had once seen of himself.

There were only one or two people in the room, sat by the exit to reception. The two bar attendants looked bored, but the air was one of peace and quiet after the chaos of the marquee.

Perry chose a table away from the lawn exit, placed Wes and Kelly on the cushioned bench seats with their backs to the wall, while she and Joe sat opposite.

"Now, Mr and Mrs Staines, if we're to get you away safely on honeymoon, we're going to have to work quickly, and you are going to have to answer me honestly. You both know Mr Murray. He'll advise you on any points you may not be sure about, and he may ask questions where I don't. You're not obliged to answer him, of course, but if you don't, then I will ask the same question and you will answer me. Do we all understand?"

"We had nothing to do with it," Wes insisted.

"Let's see if we can prove that, shall we? We're still holding Mr Drummond for further questioning, but he has told us that you both knew Mr Pitman, the victim."

Wes shook his head. "Never seen him before, never heard of him. I dunno where Rott got that from."

Perry turned to Kelly. "Mrs Staines?"

Joe noticed immediately that she was wary of speaking. Her eyes darted constantly to her new husband and back to the inspector.

"Mrs Staines, did you know Adam Pitman?"

Kelly cleared her throat. "Er, yes. I did. I knew him from my time in London."

Joe's attention transferred to Wes, whose features ran the gamut from surprise to disbelief, to suspicion and back again.

"In what capacity?" Perry asked.

"I, er, I just knew him, that's all."

The inspector pressed further. "That, Mrs Staines, is not what we have been told. In fact, our information is that, like your friend Ms Garbutt, you modelled for Pitman. Is that true?"

Kelly did not answer, and Wes's face now began to colour with anger, rising quickly through pink to violent red.

"What the bloody hell are you saying? That my wife—"

Perry silenced him with a raised hand. "I'm anxious to hear what your wife has to say, Mr Staines. Mrs Staines, would you prefer that you and I spoke in private."

"Not a good idea," Joe said, contributing for the first time. "Kelly, if you speak to the inspector in private, Wes will only demand to hear what's gone on and that could make any argument even worse. Just answer Ms Perry."

Kelly clearly did not want to answer. Her colour rose, too, and Joe noticed her hands shaking. She pressed them to the tabletop in an effort to hide the trembling. Her eye movements increased, darting this way and that, as if she were seeking some kind of escape.

"Mrs Staines, I must insist on an answer."

"Kelly, this needs to come out," Joe told her. "No one is

going to hold anything against you. Certainly not Wes, and not me or the inspector, and, as long as everything is above board, it'll go no further than us four. Did you pose for Pitman?"

She nodded. It was the tiniest movement of her head, but it was sufficient to break the deadlock.

"Good," Perry said. "There's obviously something about this business which you don't want to talk about, but I have to know everything so I can decide if it has a bearing on today's events. Did you have a relationship with this man?"

"No!"

The answer was bitten off, a defensive denial, and it came so quickly that Joe knew that it was the truth.

"Darlene was the one he was sleeping with. Not me."

"Then why were you so reluctant to answer?" Joe asked, and the answer occurred to him right away. "This modelling; it wasn't clothing, was it?"

He noticed that Wes had calmed a little after Kelly denied any relationship with Pitman, but now, as Joe's innuendo struck home, his colour came back, and his anger returned.

Kelly sucked in her breath and in a shaky voice, answered. "No. It was what's known as glamour work. Nude modelling for magazines."

\*\*\*

"Ah, there you are. Determined to get drunk, are you?"

In the light of Sheila's accusation, Brenda pushed away her glass of Campari. "No, I am not getting drunk. I'm bloody annoyed. And before you ask, yes, I am annoyed with Joe."

Sheila pulled up a chair and sat alongside her best friend. "Why?"

"How many times have we been in this same situation? Remember when George Robson was arrested at the Regency in Leeds? Remember when the police interviewed me in

Chester? What did Joe do? He fought tooth and nail for us. Now what is he doing? A newlywed couple, the son of one of our friends, and he's helping the bloody police to prevent them going off on their honeymoon. He's a bloody Judas. And why? Cos he fancies that bag, Perry?"

Sheila sipped on a gin and tonic. "I don't know that that's true. He's given no indication that he finds her, er, attractive, but even if he did, he wouldn't let that interfere. The police, Brenda, are doing their job. If there is a suspicion that either Wes or his wife were mixed up in this, then they cannot be allowed to leave." She put her glass down. "Or is this simply jealousy because you were looking forward to spending the night with Joe?"

Brenda drew her glass to her again and took a healthy slug. "Don't be silly. I've never had a jealous bone in my body, and besides, whatever Joe and I had is cooling off. Sharpish. I am angry with him. He's letting down his friends."

"Nonsense."

"He is—"

"He's doing nothing of the kind, and if you took off your wedding hat, you'd know it. He is in there now, with Perry and the couple, trying to find something, anything that will clear them, and let them get away." Sheila's ire rose further. "Even Alec understands what's going on and normally, he knows nothing more than painting and decorating and the demands of his hormones. What has Joe had in return? A heap of abuse from Julia, and more abuse from you. How has he responded? He didn't fight back. He didn't even lose his temper with either of you, which is very unusual for Joe. And why? Because he's more concerned for that couple."

"You're getting sweet on him now, are you?"

It was a silly, childish accusation, fuelled by drink and anger, but it helped calm Sheila.

"Oh, grow up, Brenda." She took another wet from her glass. "You and I have been friends all our lives. We should be

59

able to talk to one another plainly. We should be able to tell each other when we're getting it wrong, and right now, you're getting it wrong."

"Joe is a friend too… or he was. Shouldn't we be telling him when he's getting it wrong?"

"Of course we should, and we do. But right now, Brenda, he isn't getting it wrong. You are. And so is Julia. You hurt him when all he's trying is his best."

"Hurt him? My eye. You couldn't hurt him with a sledgehammer to his head."

Sheila shook her head and sighed. "And I always thought you understood people better than me. There's more here than you're telling me but you're wrong, Brenda. Completely wrong."

\*\*\*

Wes was on his feet, shouting. "You took your clothes off and let that pervert photograph you?"

Alongside him, Kelly was in tears again. On the opposite side of the table, Joe watched their reactions closely while Perry made an effort to soothe the waters.

"Please sit down, Mr Staines."

"Sod off," Wes snapped. "I just married her and now I'm finding out what a bloody tart she's been."

"Wes, you're behaving like a total prat," Joe warned him, "and this won't get you on your plane."

"We won't be getting on any plane," he shouted, attracting the attention of the bar staff. "There won't be any honeymoon. And I'm beginning to wish there hadn't been a wedding."

He stormed away and through the exit to the lawns.

"Wes…" Kelly pleaded after him.

She too stood up, but Joe stayed her.

"Take a tip, chicken, don't go near him yet. He needs a few minutes to calm down."

"It's ruined," Kelly wept. "Everything is ruined. And all through that little…"

She sat down, and buried her face in her hands.

Joe got to his feet. "I'll get her a drink. You want anything?"

"Vodka and tonic would be handy," Perry said.

As Joe reached the bar, Nelson hurried in. "Ah, Mr Murray. I've just had a call from my bar staff about a disturbance between you and your friends."

"A small brandy, a vodka and tonic and a half of bitter," Joe ordered, then turned his attention to the manager. "The friend with her back to us is Detective Inspector Perry of Cumbria police. Would you like to complain to her?"

Nelson blanched. "Detective… Oh. Oh dear. I see… well… er, in that, er, in that case, perhaps I'd better…"

"Mind your own business," Joe suggested when Nelson trailed off, lost for words.

"Right. I'll get back to reception."

"I'm sorry, sir," Storm said as Nelson's back retreated out of the room. "I didn't realise you were with plod."

"No worries, lad." Joe pointed again at Perry as Storm placed the drinks on the bar. "Chalk it up to room eleven, sport. Oh. Hey. You're still here at this time. Have you been on duty all day?"

"I came on at half ten this morning, went off at one o'clock and came back on at eight, and I'll be here until about one in the morning."

"And they talk about slave labour. I have my own business and even my people don't work those kinda hours."

Storm smiled. "I'm a temp, Mr Murray, drafted in to cope with today's rush. I could do with more permanent work, and I have to show willing, but right now, I need the money."

"That's what I like to hear. Willingness to work."

Joe picked up the drinks and returned to the table, where he found Kelly a little calmer.

"Here, chicken. Get that down you." He sat down and

sipped at his beer. "Wes obviously didn't know, did he?"

Kelly shook her head and gulped down some brandy. "I've never told anyone."

"Were you ashamed or something?" Perry asked.

"Shame isn't the right word," Kelly replied and toyed with the glass. "I'm a primary school teacher. Do you have any idea what might happen if it got out?"

"Why not start the beginning?" Joe suggested. "How did you get involved with Pitman?"

A brief silence followed. Joe assumed she was putting the tale together in her head. He guessed that Perry understood it, too, for she remained silent.

"We were students, Darlene and I. Teacher training. Pitman was there, too, studying media with the emphasis on visuals. Photography. He put up a notice for models. Male and female. He was offering payment. Like all students we were strapped for cash, so we went along. When he told us it would be nude work, I backed out, but Darlene didn't care. All she could think about was a few hundred pounds for the work. In the end he paid her fifty pounds, and she only got that because he sold the work to a, er, lads' magazine. You know the kind of thing I mean."

"I think I can remember," Joe said, and Perry smiled for the first time that evening. "So how did you get involved?"

"When Darlene came back, she told me how good he was. Didn't touch her or anything. Absolutely professional. So I took the chance, and I made fifty pounds on the deal, just like her but he only paid me after he'd been paid by the same lads' magazine. I forgot about it afterwards, but Darlene wanted more, so she kept on badgering him. Eventually, they got into a relationship. She was with him for about two years, as I remember. Then it all went sour, she moved out. And the next thing I knew, she turned up here. Wanted to get away from London and away from Pitman."

Joe's memory clicked into place. "Was this the reason she

dropped out of teacher training?"

Kelly nodded and knocked back another slug of brandy. "She had this idea that she could make it big as a model. I think Pitman had been sweet-talking her. Naturally, she never did. It was all patter from him, designed to, er… you know."

"Get her into bed?" Joe asked, and Kelly nodded.

"Forgive me, Kelly, but you must have known how it might compromise your teaching career," Perry said.

"I was young, broke and bloody stupid," she argued. "I'd have done anything for a few pounds, bar selling myself. Besides, the magazine he sold the pictures to, went bust years ago. The chances of those pictures turning up were remote, so I just shut up about it, and now, thanks to you two, everyone will know. I'm finished."

She began to cry again.

"No one else need know," Joe assured her.

"No? You think Wes will be slow to tell them? He'll tell his mother for sure, and she doesn't like me, so she'll be happy to spread it about."

"Julia's not like that," he tried to tell her.

"She wasn't slow to punch you."

"She was aiming at her." Joe pointed to Perry. "I just got in the way. Now come on, Kelly, it's time to grin and bear it. We'll minimise the damage somehow. For now, tell us where you and Wes were this afternoon."

"Our room. I was tired, and half cut after the reception. It'd been a long day, and I needed some rest. I slept for a couple of hours."

"And Wes?" Perry asked.

"He was with me at first. I know he got changed and went out for a smoke and breath of air, but I don't think he was gone long. Half an hour at the most."

"What time would that be?"

"Oh, I don't know. About six-ish. Maybe earlier."

"And you never left the room?"

Kelly glowered at Perry. "I told you. No. Look, I don't know who killed Adam, but it wasn't me, and it can't have been Wes."

"Why not?"

Perry, Joe noticed, was becoming the hardnosed police officer again.

"Why would he?" Kelly demanded. "He didn't know that I had any history with Adam, so he had no motive to kill him."

"Did Darlene?" Joe asked.

"Well, she was certainly hard on him, but she's not like that, Mr Murray. She's not vicious."

"What about her brothers?" the inspector asked.

"Jezz and Ricky? Pair of nutters, for sure, but I wouldn't think they were killers. I don't know. You'd have to speak to them."

Perry closed her notebook. "All right, Kelly, you can go back to your party."

"Will we be able to, you know, go on honeymoon?"

Perry smiled encouragingly. "I'm about to discuss that with my constable. I'll let you know soon, I promise."

Kelly got to her feet. "That's if there is a honeymoon."

They watched her leave the room.

"Poor girl," Perry said, putting her phone to her ear and calling Lesney.

"Bad start to married life," Joe agreed. "And people criticise me for being up front and outspoken. At least I don't have secrets from those who matter."

Perry finished her brief call and dropped her phone in her bag. "So, what does Joe Murray think?"

"I think you should let those two kids go to the Maldives. Wes's reaction, when he learned of Kelly's history with Pitman, looked genuine to me, in which case, he had no axe to grind with Pitman. And you said you doubted that a woman could have hanged Pitman alone, in which case, Kelly is unlikely to have done it."

"I actually said I was keeping an open mind on whether a woman could have done it. I'm sorry, Joe, but I can't forget that very history of which Wes knew nothing. It's a valid motive for killing Pitman, and Kelly could well have struck the blow, and while she may look frail and slender, she could have the strength to lift him and hang him by his camera strap."

"So that means Wes and Kelly don't get away?"

"I'm weighing the pros and cons," Perry insisted.

Lesney joined them, giving a brief rundown of her conversation with Darlene. When the constable had finished, Perry paused a moment to absorb the information and then looked to Joe.

"Darlene's told you next to nothing," Joe summarised, "other than she was sleeping with Rott for most of the afternoon, but I'll ask something neither Darlene nor Kelly have told any of us. How the hell did Pitman know the wedding would be here?"

"Well, if he really was stalking Darlene, it wouldn't be difficult to find out, sir," Lesney said.

"We were discussing that very point earlier, if you remember, Joe," Perry pointed out. "Windermere is a small town. It wouldn't be difficult to find out where the wedding is."

"No, you don't understand. What I mean is, how did Pitman know Wes and Kelly were getting married and how did he know Darlene would be a bridesmaid? Yes, I remember you saying it could be her brothers opening their mouths, but I saw the spat between them. If they knew Pitman, and it's ten to one they did, he wouldn't go anywhere near them, even in London. There has to be something more. Something that told Pitman to be here in Windermere today."

"You're making it sound as if he was invited to his death."

Joe grimaced. "That's exactly what I'm thinking."

# Chapter Six

It was a few minutes after midnight when Joe and the two police officers stepped back into the marquee.

Some guests were dancing, half heartedly, to slow music from the DJ. Most people were sitting around in cliques. Kelly, he noted, was with her parents, and Wes was several tables away with his parents, Sheila and Brenda. Lee and Cheryl were close by, and Danny was asleep on Cheryl's knee.

The moment Joe entered, Alec Staines made a beeline for him. "Joe, what the hell is going on? Wes came out of there half an hour ago on his own and he won't tell us what's gone on. Kelly turned up ten minutes back, and she won't say either. They're not speaking to one another and when I asked Wes whether he can go on honeymoon, he told me to forget it. What is happening?"

Joe referred him to Inspector Perry.

"It goes against my better judgement, Mr Staines, but I think we can allow your son and daughter-in-law to take their honeymoon. I may have to place some conditions on it, but they will be enforced only when they get back."

"Great, shall I tell them or will you? Or shall we both do it? I'll tell our Wes, and you can tell Kelly, cos right now, like I just said, they're not even speaking to one another."

"Alec," Joe intervened, "if Wes hasn't told you what went on, then I can't either. It's a matter of some confidence, and it's really nothing to do with anyone but him and his wife. But I'll tell you what I'll do with you. Let Inspector Perry deliver the good news to Kelly, and I'll talk to Wes... alone. I think I may be able to get him to see sense."

"No disrespect, Joe, but you've never had kids. How can—"

"I brought Lee up, didn't I? His mother was never interested in him after she brought him back from Oz. Let me speak to the lad."

Alec shrugged. "All right. If you can put it right, be my guest."

They split up, Perry making for Kelly and her party, Joe and Alec walking towards Wes. As he approached, Julia pointed an angry, shaking finger at Joe.

"Get away from us. I don't want you anywhere near me or my son."

Joe ignored her. "Wes, come with me and let's get a beer."

Julia stood. "Did you hear me? I said—"

"I think they can hear you in Carlisle, Julia," Joe interrupted, "but I'm not talking to you. I'm talking to Wes."

"You evil little—"

"Julia," Alec barked. "Shut up."

Everyone was shocked into momentary silence. All eyes turned on the mother and father of the groom. Even Wes lifted his head.

"Thirty odd years and hardly a cross word between us, and now look at you. You're carrying on like a bloody witch, and you're going too far. Joe is trying to help. Now, for God's sake bite your tongue."

Julia gaped, others turned half away, eager to eavesdrop yet keen to distance themselves from the battle between man and wife.

Joe felt embarrassed for Julia and Alec, but he suppressed his feelings and addressed Wes again. "Come on, lad. Let's go get a pint on our own."

"Mr Murray, I know you mean well, but I really don't feel like it."

"I know you don't, and quite honestly, I could do with getting off to bed, but it'll be worth your while. Come on.

Let's go to the bar."

Joe turned and walked to the marquee exit. From behind, he heard Alec encouraging his son.

"Go with him, Wes. It can't do any harm, can it?"

A moon just past full bathed the hotel in ghostly light when Joe emerged from the bar carrying two beers, and sat at an outside table with Wes. He took out his tobacco, rolled a cigarette, lit it and suffered the usual coughing fit, before relaxing and savouring the warm night air.

"What was it you said earlier today? Wouldn't it be great if it could be like this all the time?"

Wes, too, lit a smoke and snorted derisively. "Did I say that?"

"Summat like it," Joe said and pulled on his cigarette again. "Trouble is, Wes, life isn't like this all the time, and in its own way, that's a good thing. You need the bad now and then, otherwise how would you know when you were happy?"

"Yeah, like it's exactly what you need on your wedding day, innit? A good dose of misery to let you know how happy you'll be one day."

Joe puffed contentedly on his cigarette. "I do have some good news. Perry will let you go tomorrow. You can take Kelly off to the Maldives and have your week of sun, sand and, er, whatever else you young people get up to."

"Not interested. She can go to hell."

"And waste a perfectly good holiday?"

"I'll stand it," Wes declared. "Maybe I can send Mum and Dad."

Joe chuckled. "I'm sure they'd love it. But I'm also sure they'd love it more if you and your new wife got on that plane."

"It's not gonna happen." Wes's anger had begun to rise again.

Joe sipped his beer and enjoyed the tang. "Tell me what bothers you, Wes? The fact that Kelly didn't tell you about it, or the fact that she did it."

"What do you think?"

"I already know what I think," Joe retorted. "I think you're behaving like a total prat, but I need to know *why* you're behaving like a total prat."

"She did it. Right?" Wes bit the words off. "She took all her clothes off for some geek with a camera and let him sell the pictures to a magazine. How many sad sacks have been drooling over her while they played with themselves? Huh? Answer me that. My wife, showing all she's got for these..." he trailed off and fumed at the night, pulling angrily on his cigarette.

Joe allowed a moment's silence and took the time to enjoy another lungful of tobacco smoke, followed by another mouthful of beer.

"How long have you been together? Lived together, I mean."

Wes had been staring moodily at the inset lights on the lawns. Joe's question brought his attention back. "Oh. About two years. Maybe a bit more." The anger split his features again. "And she never told me anything about it."

"Hmm, I know that, and even if I didn't it wouldn't take a genius to work it out from your reaction. I was thinking along different lines, though. Did you ever go on holiday in that two years? You know, proper holidays. Spain and the like."

"Yeah. Course we did."

"And did Kelly do any sunbathing?"

"Yeah. What of it?"

"Topless sunbathing?"

"Well, yes. A bit. Where she was allowed.

Joe looked Wes in the eye. "Did that bother you?"

"No. But it's different, isn't it?"

"Is it? You know, Wes, when I married Alison – you remember Alison, don't you – we went to Spain for our honeymoon, and before she got a touch of Spanish tummy, we did a bit of sunbathing on the beach at Lloret. She took her top off, too. She wasn't the only one. Almost every woman on the beach was topless. I didn't know where to look to avoid the pap."

Wes tried to suppress a smile. "I know what you mean."

"I hid behind my sunglasses and tried not to look."

Wes was quiet for a moment. "What's your point?"

"My point is, I hid behind my sunglasses. How many other blokes did the same? And later, how many of those other blokes went back to their hotels and got off on what they'd been ogling? The same applies to you? When you were on holiday, how many other blokes ogled Kelly when she was sunbathing, and how many of them were getting off on it?"

"I don't know." The answer came out defiant and defensive.

"And it never bothered you. Yet she appeared in a magazine, which she tells me has gone out of print, flashing her bits and that troubles you."

"It's different."

"It's not different, and she has valid reasons for not telling anyone. The same reason she didn't bring topless photographs back from Majorca or Tenerife or wherever you went. She's a primary school teacher. She has to be discreet. Young men and women like her lead double lives. They can go out and get tanked up the same as we can, but they can't get into bother over it in case the little kiddies find out. They can sow their wild oats, but not in the back fields where some jerk leading the kids on a nature ramble might stumble on them. You're a plumber and gas fitter. Who gives a toss if you show up starkers in the centrefold of Playgirl? She's a teacher. It could cost her her job. She did what she did at a time when she was strapped for cash. To her it was a business deal. For fifty quid, I'd stand naked as Mr November in the Catering Services Calendar, and as long as I profited, I wouldn't give a hoot who said what, but Kelly isn't me and she isn't you."

Wes remained silent, and Joe felt his anger rising.

"Right now, she's in there terrified that she's hurt you, or more likely hurt your pride. She's fallen off that pedestal you put her on. She doesn't need you behaving like a childish pillock. She needs you in there, where she can talk to you, get it out of her system, maybe even apologise for it, although I don't know what she has to apologise for. Whatever the hell, she needs you there. She needs to know you're on her side and not that of some lecher with a camera who got his head smashed in. Now use your loaf, lad. Get in there, drag off to one side, tell her how much she really means to you and get it put right. And when you've done that, put her in your car and take her off to Manchester Airport and get on that plane. You have two weeks in the Indian Ocean to enjoy yourself, and the rest of your life to sort out your petty squabbles. Right?"

There was a significant pause before Wes nodded, got to his feet and walked slowly towards the marquee.

Joe dragged on his cigarette again, satisfied with his work.

The clank of bottles and glasses from behind alerted him. He looked over his shoulder, where Storm was clearing the debris of the afternoon and evening.

"Everything all right, sir?"

"I hope so, lad. How about you?"

He yawned. "Just tidying up before I call it a night."

"Well, if you need a reference to get you that permanent job, refer them to me."

Storm grinned. "I'll do that." He took Wes's empty glass. "Cops found who did it, yet?"

"Bit early for that, Storm. These things take time." Joe drained his glass, and handed it to the barman. "You get a good night's sleep… when you can."

"Thanks. I'll try."

Joe ambled back towards the marquee. Stepping in, he noticed right away that Wes had taken Kelly off to one side and they were deep in conversation. Alec and Julia Staines were also talking earnestly, the police were comparing notes,

71

and Sheila was with Lee and Cheryl, while Brenda appeared to be asleep at the next table.

He crossed to the police officers. "If you two are through for the night, I'm gonna shoot off to bed."

Perry nodded. "We'll be back first thing in the morning, Joe. We'll need to interview everyone here. Purely routine, you understand."

"Of course. And Rott?"

"We'll be questioning Mr Drummond again in the morning."

"If you get anything from your forensic people, you'll let me know?"

"I promise. And if you come across anything—"

"You'll be the first to hear." Joe yawned. "Right. Time I was off to me bed. See you tomorrow."

From the police, he wandered across the floor and joined Sheila, just as Lee and Cheryl were leaving.

Bidding Lee and Cheryl goodnight, Sheila eyed Wes and Kelly. "I don't know what you said, Joe, but it seems to have done the trick."

"Kicked his backside and made him realise how selfish he's being."

"I have to say as weddings go, I've been to happier events," Sheila said. "You do know this will haunt them for the rest of their lives. I do hope it's not an omen."

"I don't believe in omens, Sheila. You make your own luck, or lack of it, in this life." He glanced across at Brenda. "Blathered?"

Sheila shook her head. "Tired. That's all. What's the state of the investigation?"

"As I just told Storm, the barman, it's up in the air." He frowned. "Like all killings, the way forward lies with the victim, and right now we have a lot of contradictory evidence coming in. Darlene says Pitman was harassing her, Pitman said she was harassing him, and I can't understand how he knew that the wedding was on and that Darlene would be here. Even if he knew, what the hell made him think it would be safe to turn up here? Certain things – I can't tell you what – point to Kelly as a possible suspect, but I managed to persuade Perry that Wes's hurt feelings were not an act, and at least they can get away in the morning." Joe yawned again and checked his watch. "A quarter to one, and I need some sleep. Clear my brain. Need a hand with Brenda?"

Sheila shook her head. "I told you she's tired, not smashed. I think we all are."

"In that case, it's really time for the land of nod. I'll see you for breakfast."

# Chapter Seven

The view from Joe's window at eight the following morning was of the lake and hills beyond bathed in glorious sunshine, the hotel casting sharp edged shadows on the lawns below.

He had fallen asleep the moment his head hit the pillow, and slept for a solid six hours. Awake and refreshed, after making a cup of tea and throwing open the windows, he felt invigorated, ready to face the challenges of the day.

Stepping out onto the tiny balcony, ignoring the sign reading, 'For the benefit of other guests please refrain from smoking', he lit his first cigarette of the day and promptly wished he hadn't. The smoke bit into his lungs, forcing him to cough, and he found it hard to loosen the deeply buried phlegm.

"You bloody idiot," he cursed himself.

Smoking had never been a big issue for him. He smoked; end of debate. He knew the arguments for and against, and they did nothing to persuade him. But his current breathing troubles, seemingly getting worse by the day, told him it was time to address the matter; time to stop before it killed him.

But not today. Today, on top of the proposed visit to Hilltop Farm, he had the problem of Adam Pitman's death to deal with, and he had many questions outstanding.

After finishing his tea and smoke, washing up the cup, he showered and dressed in his shorts and a clean T-shirt (muttering mutinously on the prospect of another confrontation with Harriet Atkinson) and putting on his ubiquitous gilet, made his way downstairs for breakfast.

Taking his seat alongside a cheerful Sheila and morose Brenda, he greeted them both with a grunt that could have been 'good morning' or 'leave me alone', and looked around the Donald Campbell Room.

Most of the wedding party were there, but the Staineses were a notable exception.

"Alec and Julia went with Wes and Kelly to Manchester. See them off on their honeymoon," Sheila explained. "Kelly's parents went with them. Alec told me last night, but he also said they have to come back so the police can interview them."

"They'll need to talk to everyone," Joe said, taking a glass of orange juice from the waiter and ordering a full English breakfast. "It's pure formality. And I need to speak to one or two people today, before they go home."

"So do I," Brenda said. "I need to speak to you, Joe."

"Funny. I thought you said enough last night."

She stared gloomily down at her cup of tea. "I was wrong. I'm sorry."

"And you should be. You seriously thought I would take the cops' side in this?"

"You did. You said they were right."

"Only because they were," Joe argued. "Wedding or no wedding, and whether Pitman deserved it or not, he was murdered, and you know the score. Everyone is a suspect until the police can eliminate them."

In an obvious effort to pour oil on troubled waters, Sheila said, "Wes and Kelly are still suspects, aren't they?"

Joe nodded and sipped his juice, the tart fluid biting into his taste buds, and causing him to screw up his face. "Not serious suspects or they wouldn't be on their way to the Indian Ocean, but yes, they're still on the list." He glanced across the room at Darlene and her brothers. "I need to speak with those three. I can't understand how Pitman knew to be here. I don't care what Perry and her constable have to say, someone must have tipped him off."

Sheila perked up, her face registering surprise. She exchanged a glance with Brenda, and asked, "Are you saying he was lured here, Joe?"

"In a manner of speaking, yes. I'm not saying whoever brought him here intended to kill him. I'm simply saying he was encouraged to turn up here, and if we can learn who did that, then we're on our way to finding his killer."

The waiter returned with Joe's breakfast, and he attacked it with gusto.

"Lee and Cheryl are taking Danny to Hilltop Farm today. Beatrix Potter's home," Sheila said. "We're going with them. Are you coming?"

That Sheila was doing most of the talking was not lost on Joe. Brenda sat opposite him, taking serious interest in a bowl of cornflakes.

He nodded at Sheila. "Might as well. Nothing better to do, have I?" He eyed Darlene and her brothers again. "Not after I've spoken to them three, I haven't."

Twenty minutes later, after finishing breakfast and rolling his second cigarette of the day, he excused himself, left the table and ambled across to Darlene and her brothers.

"You busy?"

She scowled back. "Who's asking?"

"I am, because I need to speak to you." Joe's determined stare took in both her brothers. "All three of you."

"We already spoke to the filth," Jezz said.

"I know you did, but they're lame, aren't they? They never ask the right questions. I do."

"Just push off, granddad," Ricky warned. "We don't have to talk to you."

"True, but if you don't I might just speak to Perry and tell her a bit more of what I saw yesterday. I might even tell her about the way you threatened me." His words were having no effect, so he changed direction. "Y'see, sunbeam, they're looking for someone who has a grudge against Pitman, and someone strong enough to lift his body and hang it. She has the grudge." He pointed at Darlene, "but no way could she lift his body up. You two could, though." He held up his cigarette. "I'll be outside having a smoke. Don't be long. I've a waterbus to catch."

Joe walked away, out into the lobby and cut through the Beatrix Potter Room out onto the lawns, where he commandeered an empty table, sat down, and lit his cigarette. He never once looked back to see whether they had followed him, but he was not surprised when they came out of the hotel and joined him.

Jezz, the larger of the two brothers went on the attack.

"You don't know who you're dealing with, pal."

"Yes I do," Joe argued. "A pair of playground bullies. In truth, lad, it's the other way round. *You* don't know who *you're* dealing with. I'm Joe Murray, and I have police contacts all over the country, and if you want to call my bluff, go ahead. I'll have you two walled up before dinner, and it doesn't matter if what I'm telling the law is the truth or not. They're looking into a murder and they'll lock you up with Rott just to be on the safe side."

"We had nothing to do with it," Ricky protested.

"Maybe, maybe not. Talk to me, and we'll maybe prove that. Now sit down, all of you." He half turned in his chair, and faced Darlene as she took a seat beside him. "Tell me about Adam Pitman and you, and before you try telling me load of porkies, I already know most of it. I wanna hear it from you."

Darlene's cheeks coloured. "There was no me and Adam Pitman. Well, not recently there wasn't."

"I know about the modelling," Joe told her. "Kelly said you had a thing with him, then, when it went wrong, you moved up here to get away from him. That true?"

She nodded. "It's one of them things, isn't it? It was good for a while, but then I realised he was just a daydreamer, who'd never amount to anything, so I called it a draw. But he kept pestering me, so I moved up here."

"You didn't sick these two onto him?" Joe indicated her brothers.

Jezz and Ricky were quick to protest but Darlene silenced them with a glower and a warning. "Shut it. Right? I'm talking." She turned back to Joe. "Do you know what Adam was really interested in? Me taking my kit off and posing for soft porn mags. When I met him he was all over me, telling me how I could make it in the modelling game – clothed and unclothed – and like an idiot I fell for it. Fell for him. I even gave up college for him, but every time we did a shoot, I was always naked. I got sick of it, told him I'd had enough and walked. But he wouldn't let it go. Kept coming round to my place, badgering me. In the end, I got in touch with Kelly and she suggested I move up here, out of his reach."

"And he didn't know where you were?" Joe waited until she shook her head, then asked the brothers, "What price one of you let slip in a pub where Darlene was?"

Both denied it.

"We're discreet," Ricky said.

"On yesterday's performance I reckon you're as discreet as a thirty-ton truck," Joe commented, and taking a final drag on his cigarette, stubbed it out.

A few moments of coughing followed. Eventually, regaining control of his breathing, Joe apologised and said, "Yesterday, when Tweedledum and Tweedledee showed him the way out, he said you had been hassling him, yet you told the police it was the other way round. If he didn't know where you were, how could he hassle you?"

"Text messages," Darlene said. "From the day I left him he was texting me. Then they stopped for a bit, and started again about two, maybe three, months ago."

Joe pondered the timing for a moment, then, unable to make much of it, asked, "Did you keep any of the messages?"

"I just dumped them."

"And you never reported it to the police?"

"Waste of time, that is," Darlene grumbled. "He used different phones, or different SIM cards in his phone, and I knew him. The cards wouldn't have been registered. Anyway, I told that Detective Inspector yesterday and they said they'd be getting onto my phone company to see where the messages were coming from."

Joe sniffed. "That could take days, weeks even." He drummed his finger on the table, then took out his tobacco and began rolling another cigarette. "Jezz, Ricky, let's think about you two. Did you know Pitman?"

"Only through Darlene," Jezz replied.

"You didn't drink in the same pubs or anything?"

"Difficult," Ricky replied. "We're from South London; Catford, he was from East London. Barking, Dagenham way. The other side of the river."

"How did you meet him, Darlene?"

"University," she replied. "Kelly and me were doing a PGCE, and—"

"Sorry?" Joe interrupted. "PGCE?"

"Post Graduate Certificate of Education," Darlene translated. "It's your ticket into teaching after you've done a degree."

In the act of lighting his cigarette, Joe suffered another coughing fit. "You… you have a degree?" he gasped.

"You don't have to sound so surprised," Darlene complained. "I did my degree at the University of East London and went on for a fourth year for my PGCE. Kelly had been to Nottingham or Leicester or somewhere in the Midlands and she came to UEL for her PGCE. That's where we met."

"And it's where you met Pitman?"

She nodded. "He was a mature student. Bit older than most of us. About thirty at the time. He was doing some course on

79

visual media; that's photography, video, image manipulation on computers and that kinda stuff. You know what I mean."

"And he canvassed the student as models?"

"Yeah. I mean, me and Kelly, we weren't the only ones, you know." Darlene scowled. "I was just the idiot who fell for his chat."

"And you were, what, living with him?"

"For a while, yeah. Then, the year before last I came up here to stay with Wes and Kelly for a few days. She made me see him for what he really was. A lecher. Coupla months later, I dumped him and the hassle started." Darlene sighed. "I gave up everything for that git. I gave up my studies, I gave up my clothing, I gave up my dignity, I s'ppose, all on this promise of me becoming a model, and now look at me. Kelly stuck with the plan, and she's where she wants to be. I ditched it for a bloody daydream, and I'm working the checkouts in the Co-op."

"We all make mistakes, Darlene, and I'm sure you'll pick yourself up at some stage," Joe assured her. "So you dumped Pitman and moved here permanently last year, and the hassle stopped."

She nodded. "Changed my phone and everything. Got rid of my internet supplier, found another. It stopped the lot."

"Then how did he get hold of your number to start hassling you again?"

She shrugged. "It's registered. I reckon he got it from the mobile directory. He woulda known where I'd moved. The only place I'd go after London was here, and there ain't that many Darlene Garbutts in Windermere."

Joe chewed his lip. "Probably not, but it's much more likely that someone gave him your number."

"Like who? Kelly? She hated him."

"All right, not Kelly. How about boyfriends? You been involved with anyone while you've been here?"

"A few," Darlene replied diffidently. She perked up and

went on the attack. "I'm not a tart, you know. I don't just jump into bed with blokes."

"No, no. That's not what I was thinking. Did any of these guys know you'd been getting grief from Pitman?"

She shrugged again. "Coulda done. I might have talked about it."

"So if you dropped some guy and he got a bit, you know, mad over it, he might find Pitman and tell him where you were? I meanersay, if you told these blokes the tale, it wouldn't be too difficult to track him down, would it?"

"I suppose not, but I don't remember anyone being that hacked off after we finished. Most of the men round here are fine, but they spend their time moaning about how the townies and holiday letting companies have taken over the housing, and how you can't get jobs and stuff. They're all living with their parents. They're nice enough guys, but you can't get serious with them cos they're going nowhere. Kelly was lucky. She latched onto Wes, a man with his own business."

"If you'll forgive me, you didn't seem to be doing too bad with Rott, yesterday."

She smiled fondly. "Rott's mostly like Wes. Businessman, doing well for himself, and quite a catch in his own way. He's been chasing me for about three months now. We've had a coupla dates, that's all. I know he's a nutter when he loses it, but he's good fun, you know."

"I know, all right. I've known Wes and Rott since they were kids back in Sanford."

She chuckled. "He told me."

"Three months," Joe ruminated. "Just about the time when Pitman began hassling you again."

Darlene was obviously taken aback. "Well, yeah, but you can't think Rott would be behind that."

"No. No, I don't. But what about boyfriends before Rott? Someone you finished with who might have got a bit hacked off and daren't approach you because Rott was looking to

81

hitch up to you."

She shook her head. "Can't think of anyone."

Joe could think of no more to ask about her past, so he switched tack. "Okay. No problem. Tell me about yesterday afternoon. You and Rott. When I left the reception, he was well oiled. What did you do after?"

She paused a moment gathering her thoughts. "Wes booked two rooms; one for him and Rott and one for me and Kelly. After the wedding, him and Kelly, they wanted to be together, so they took the room he'd booked for him and Rott and he gave me the key for the other room. I was really hot, if you take my meaning."

Joe recalled his response to a similar question from Kelly the previous night and wondered why everyone appeared to assume he was completely over the hill?

"I think I can remember," he said. "Go on."

"But Rott got smashed. Really blasted." Darlene frowned. "I was, a bit, er, a bit annoyed at the state he got into. But you already know about that. You saw that. We got back to the room, he hit the bed and he was gone in a minute."

Joe puzzled over the information. "Is Rott on anything, do you know?"

She shrugged. "Not to my knowledge."

"And what about you?"

"I don't do drugs, Mr Murray."

Joe chuckled. "Sorry, Darlene. My fault. I didn't mean were you doing drugs. I mean what did you do when you got back to the room?"

"Oh right." Darlene appeared mollified. "Well, I was a bit frustrated, and annoyed, obviously, but I hit the mattress, too, and I fell asleep."

"And you woke up, what time?"

She shrugged. "I'm not sure. Seven, or just after."

"Y'see, Darlene, if you were out that long, for all you know, Rott could have woke up, nipped down through the bottom gate, met Pitman, killed him and been back in your room before you woke up."

"Nah. I don't believe it. He was really gone when we left the reception. I don't know how much he'd had to drink." Darlene frowned. "I didn't think it was that much, but he was really blotto."

"Coulda been an act," Joe suggested. "There's another point. If Rott was out that long, you could have slipped out, met Pitman, killed him, had your brothers hang him up, and been back here before Rott woke up."

"We keep telling you, it was nothing to do with us," Jezz grumbled.

"I'm not saying it is," Joe responded. "I'm saying it's possible. You, Darlene, and Rott, you're providing alibis for each other, and yet neither of you can say with any certainty what the other was doing." Joe stubbed out his second cigarette and began rolling a third. "I'm not accusing anyone. The cops might, but I wouldn't. Not without concrete evidence. All crimes have three aspects. Means, motive and opportunity. The means has to be decided yet. All Perry would tell me was it was a heavy implement, but a woman could have done it. You sound like you have the motive, and from what you've just told me, you also had the opportunity. Like it or not, Darlene, everything you just said to me puts you in the frame."

# Chapter Eight

Acutely aware that he was late for his rendezvous with Sheila, Brenda, Lee and family at the boat station, Joe left Darlene and her brothers, and hurried along the path across the lawns and then down towards the road. He fished out his mobile, and after debating with himself whether to call Brenda, he instead punched in the speed dial number for Sheila.

"It's me," he said when the connection was made. "Listen, I got a bit behind with Darlene and I'm well late. Why don't you lot go across and on to Hilltop Farm. I'll sort this out, then follow you."

"You're doing it again, Joe," Sheila said. "You're supposed to be relaxing and enjoying yourself, and instead you're getting tangled up in other problems."

"I am enjoying myself. Besides, I can hardly leave Rott to, er, rot in the cells, can I? I'll get the next boat across the lake and I shouldn't be more than twenty minutes behind you."

"All right, Joe. We'll see you at Hilltop Farm."

The path followed the line of trees, then, out of sight of the hotel, veered to the left towards the church. Once past the trees, Joe could see the whole of the church, its graveyard separated from the Lakeside Manor by a stone wall, topped with high railings. A woman stood the other side of the wall, taking photographs of an old gravestone.

"Determined to keep the riff raff and the undead out," he muttered as he ambled along the gravel path.

Down in the corner, where the church property met that of the hotel, he could see the gate Sheila had told him about. A simple enough iron grille affair, with a large and bulky lock. Beyond it was the main road, busy with traffic and pedestrians, and across the road, the crowded boat station. Reaching the dividing wall, he paused a moment, shading his eyes with a hand, searching for sign of Sheila, Brenda and especially Lee, amongst the crowd of people boarding one of the boats.

"Can't bloody miss him at home," he grumbled. "He's so tall."

"You could use your mobile phone again, and bell him."

The voice came from his left. He looked around and into the smiling face of the woman who had been taking photographs of the gravestone.

"How did you know I have a mobile?" he asked.

She gestured towards the trees. "I saw you talking on it when you came round the trees. You dropped it in the pocket of your vest."

"Gilet."

"Pleased to meet you, Mr Gilet."

Joe grinned and fingered the garment. "This is a gilet. I'm Joe Murray." He offered his hand through the railings, and she shook it.

"Madeleine Chester. Most people call me Maddy."

"Nice to meet you, Maddy."

Joe estimated her to be in her mid forties. A buxom blonde dressed in shorts and a skimpy top which showed a little more flesh than was good for his blood pressure. About his height as near as he could judge, her smiling eyes were shaded by a denim, plant pot hat.

Determined to show her that his powers of observation were a match for hers, he asked, "A hobby, is it? Taking pictures of old gravestones?"

Maddy laughed. "Good God, no. It's for a client."

"Right." Joe's agreement was swathed in puzzlement. "You have clients who want photographs of old gravestones? Who are they? The Draculas?"

"Could be. I'm a genealogist."

"Ah. You dabble with DNA."

Her quizzical look questioned his sanity. "No. Family trees."

He smiled. "I know. I was only joking. So, Maddy, what prompts you to look at this particular gravestone? One of your client's long lost relatives, is it?"

"It might just be. There are a number of burials recorded here bearing my client's name, and this is only one of them. I have to check the parish records to be sure. But it's all part of the service. Here. Let me give you my card."

She dug into her bag and came out with a plain, white card, handed it through the railings, and Joe studied it.

*Madeleine Chester, Genealogist.*

*Stanhead Road*

*Cragshaven, N Yorkshire.*

Underneath it were several contact numbers.

"Cragshaven? That's near Scarborough, isn't it?"

"In a little cove a few miles up the coast towards Whitby," she confirmed.

Joe was surprised. "You're a fair way from home, then."

Maddy shrugged. "The client foots the bill. I'm staying at the Waterside. How about you? You're obviously not local with an accent like that, and you must have money to burn staying at The Lakeside Manor Hotel."

"I'm from Sanford. West Yorkshire. I own a trucker's café. The Lazy Luncheonette."

"Oh, I'll bet I know it. I've been to Sanford a few times. On business, of course."

"It would have to be." Joe laughed. "Sanford is not the tourist capital of the county. Listen, Maddy, did you say you were staying at the Waterside?" He waited for her to nod, and went on, "One of your fellow guests was murdered last night."

"Yes. I know. Police were crawling all over the pub first thing this morning. Shady sort. Carried a large camera bag."

Joe nodded. "You're very observant." He checked his watch. "Fancy a drink? I could do with knowing whatever you know."

Maddy looked up into the clear sky. "I don't know much, but I do know that working in this sun is thirsty work. I'll make my way out onto the road. The Waterside is only just along the way."

While she gathered together her belongings, Joe opened the bottom gate and let himself out onto the narrow pavement. The gate clanged shut behind him, and he examined it from the outside. As he had been advised, there was an electronic set up, with a slot for the room key. Glancing back through the railings towards the hotel, the lawns climbed steeply away from the road, and he understood why Sheila and Brenda had looked so tired the previous day.

He learned that walking on the landwards side of the road was a life and death proposition. The pavement was narrow and crowded and he regularly had to step into the road to avoid people. Eventually, he crossed over, where the lakeside pavement was wider, more accommodating.

Maddy had already crossed over and met him by the boat station.

"So who were you looking for, Joe?" she asked as they walked on towards the pub.

"My nephew and friends. They're going over to Hilltop Farm. Beatrix Potter's place. I got tangled up in this murder business, and I said I'd follow them."

"Tangled up?"

He sighed as the Waterside Inn came into view along the road, its car park crowded with cars and motorcycles, a police Scientific Support van standing off to one side. "I always get involved in these things. I have a reputation for solving crimes."

"You and me, both…Wait a minute. Filey. Last summer. Were you involved in a double killing. Manageress of the Beachside Hotel, her husband and son?"

"That was me," he said with a grin. "They ran down one of my members in Sanford, then killed one of their own. I was the one who cracked it for the cops."

"I thought your name was familiar. The police mentioned you in the local papers. They got the charge reduced to manslaughter, you know."

"I didn't know," Joe admitted. "Scandalous." Poor old Knickers-off. It should have been murder"

As they neared the pub, a police officer, suited up in white, forensic overalls, appeared, and dropped a storage box into the van.

Maddy laughed deliciously. "Knickers Off? What kind of name is that?"

"Sorry," Joe grunted. "Pet name. Knickers-off Nicola Leach. She was a member of our club. Had a habit of jumping any man who had enough money to keep her in beer."

Maddy disregarded his opinion of Nicola. "Your club?"

While she led the way past the police van, and into the Waterside, Joe went on to explain the Sanford 3rd Age Club, its workings and his role.

"Sound like fun," she said as they pressed into the crowded bar.

With low ceilings and walls adorned with pictures of the area and its famous people, the place was packed with people whom Joe assumed were mostly tourists. The four people behind the bar were rushed off their feet trying to keep up, and he noticed that little in the way of soft drinks were passing over.

"Plenty of drunk driving convictions today, I'll bet," he muttered, pushing his way between a clutch of leather-clad bikers to signal for service.

Half a dozen people were dashing about behind the bar. Joe recognised Vetch and his son, and he also thought he saw Storm at the far end of the bar, but before he could call out, the young man had disappeared into the cellar, to put a new barrel on.

Eventually, he secured a half of lager for himself and a vodka and tonic for Maddy, and they moved from the crowded, cramped interior, out into the rear beer garden where the tables were shaded under parasols jammed into old, wooden beer barrels, and the lawns meandered beneath trees to the water's edge. The sun was behind the pub now, and their table took advantage of the shade afforded by the building.

"The 3rd Age Club idea was fun and most of the time we have fun, but managing it can be a nightmare. Old timers are no different to teenagers, you know, except they have more money." He took a sip of lager and began to roll a cigarette. "Enough about me. I'm more concerned with Pitman's killing."

"I don't know that I can help you, Joe," Maddy replied. "I got here on Thursday morning, and he turned up in the evening. I was in the bar when he arrived, and I saw him about an hour later, but he wasn't the kind of man who would interest me, so other than bog standard people watching, I didn't take a lot of notice of him and his friend."

Joe's ears pricked up. "Friend?"

Putting the glass to her lips, she nodded. "Hmm." She took a swallow of the clear liquid, placed the glass on the table and turned it through her fingers. "The landlord's son. Big bugger. You know. All muscle and low forehead. Looks like he stalled a bit lower down the evolutionary scale than the rest of us."

"His name is Carl." Joe jammed the cigarette into his mouth and fished into the pockets of his gilet. "Excuse me a minute."

He came out with his lighter and a compact camera. Lighting the cigarette, going through the usual coughing routine, he powered up the camera, called up the library, and began to flick through the images until he came to one of bride, groom, best man, and bridesmaid together. He passed the camera to Maddy.

"You're sure it was Carl , and not this guy? Not the groom, the best man?"

Maddy screwed up her eyes and shaded the camera against the strong sunlight. Joe watched her brow crease as she studied the thumbnail image. Eventually, she passed it back.

"Not him. It's hard to say from that picture, and I didn't take too much notice, but I'm sure it was Carl. Why not ask him?"

"I'll check with him in a minute." Joe sipped his lager again and blew a thin stream of smoke into the morning air.

"Is he the suspect?" Maddy asked. "The man in the picture, I mean. Not Carl?"

"He's been arrested, for sure," Joe said. "But I've known Rott all his life and he's a bad-tempered so and so, but he's not a killer."

"Sorry? Rott, did you say? Odd name?"

"It's a feature of Sanford," Joe told her. "We give everyone pet names. Knickers-off, Rott is short for Rottweiler because he behaves like a rottie."

She laughed. "What's your nickname, then?"

"I have a few. Grumpy Joe and old misery guts are the most common, and they're also the ones you can safely repeat in polite company." He frowned and pulled them back on topic. "I can't work out what Rott would be doing having a beer with Pitman the night before last. When Pitman turned up at the wedding yesterday, Rott was fit to tear him to pieces."

"I don't say they were having a beer together," Maddy said. "I saw them talking, and it was pretty deep stuff, judging from their body language and Pitman's serious face. He looked quite angry now and then."

"You described them as friends," Joe pointed out.

"A generalisation," Maddy admitted. "I meant they were sitting together in the bar and talking."

"You know, for someone who didn't take a lot of notice,

you're sure giving me food for thought."

She chuckled. "I keep my eyes open, Joe, and I don't miss much. That's all. Some people think I'm a nosy mare, but you'd be surprised what you can learn if you just keep your wits about you."

As far as Joe was concerned, she was preaching to the choir, and he let the debate go. "Have you heard anything about what the police found in Pitman's room?"

"Nothing…" Maddy trailed off. "Well, just a whisper that they found some drugs. Doesn't surprise me. He looked that sort."

"Who told you that?"

"Waitress at breakfast. Gossip, I should think. Scuttlebutt. I don't think the police will have actually said anything to them. It might be something they overheard and then drew the wrong conclusion."

Again Joe was surprised. "Wrong conclusion?"

"Hmm. They hear the word drugs, and jump to the obvious conclusion, but it doesn't make it the right one."

"It doesn't?" If Joe sounded cynically sceptical, it was because he felt cynically sceptical.

"Of course not," Maddy argued. "I take drugs."

"You do?"

She smiled naughtily. "They're called Ramipril, and they lower my blood pressure."

Joe's face split into a broad grin. "Very clever. So we don't know that the police did find drugs in the room?"

"You'd have to ask the cops," Maddy advised. "So what are you trying to do, Joe? Get your friendly guard dog off the hook?"

"Not necessarily." He shrugged. "If Rott killed this man, then he should suffer. But there are things which don't make sense, and while the law are happy to accept whatever information I can give them, they're not so forthcoming with information they have." He gazed across the lake to the hills, bathed in glorious sunshine, but his mind was not focussed on the weather. "What would Rott be doing meeting Pitman? Unless it was to do with Darlene."

"Darlene?" Maddy asked.

"She's the only thing they have in common."

Joe went into detail on events at the Lakeside Manor the previous afternoon and evening, and his discussion with Darlene and her brothers an hour previously. Maddy listened, occasionally asking questions to clarify minor points, and when he had finished, she downed the rest of her drink, signalling to Joe that their business was all but over.

"I was in that church and the graveyard most of yesterday," she said, "and I saw lots of people coming and going, but I couldn't swear that I didn't see your friend, or this young woman. But I can swear that I didn't see Pitman. I would have recognised him."

"He wasn't staying at the Lakeside Manor," Joe told her. "He wouldn't have been able to get in through the bottom gate."

"No, but he could have got out," Maddy replied. "The lock is a one-way thing, isn't it? You only need the key when you're getting in from the road. Not that I can see what bearing that would have on the matter. It sounds to me, Joe, like he was lured to his death, and if the cops really did find drugs in his room..." She trailed off, leaving the idea to percolate in Joe's head.

"Point taken." He finished his lager and checked the time. "Twenty past eleven. I'd better get the boat across the lake, and join my friends. I'll have a quick word with Carl Vetch first."

They moved back into the cramped and crowded bar. Joe edged his way to the front of the packed room, where a familiar face stood under a picture of Sir Donald Campbell.

"Hello, Storm," he said. "I thought I'd seen you earlier. What are you doing here?"

"Hello, Mr Murray," Storm replied, concentrating on the

pint of lager he was pulling. "Working is what I'm doing, sir. I told you, I'm a temp. I work where and when I can. I'm back at the Lakeside this evening and tomorrow."

"Yeah. Right. It's the only way, lad."

Storm put the glass in front of his customer, took money, and there was a delay before he came back to Joe. "Now, Mr Murray, what can I get you?"

Joe pointed along the bar, to where the Bernard and Carl Vetch were chatting with customers while his staff of three hurried around serving thirsty patrons. "You can get me a word with your boss and his son, if they can spare me a minute."

"Nice kid," Maddy commented as Storm hurried off down the bar. "Dishy. He served me on Thursday night."

"Dishy?" Joe grinned.

"Too young for me, but I think my daughter would fancy him."

"He's good at his job," Joe agreed, "and that's what you need when you're running this kind of hike."

Storm spoke briefly to the landlord. Glances came Joe's way, the older man nodded, and Storm resumed his duties. The landlord carried on talking to his customer for another few moments, then made his excuse and he and his son ambled along the bar to Joe.

A tall, broad shouldered man in his early forties, his florid complexion was matched by his bulging abdomen. Joe had seen the signs in so many of his catering peers: men and women too fond of their own cooking, or in this case, his own liquid refreshments.

"Mr Murray, is it? You were at the wedding yesterday. What can I do for you?"

"Adam Pitman, the guy who was murdered, was in here night before last speaking to your son, according to Ms Chester, here." He eyed the younger Vetch. "Can you tell me what you were talking about, Carl?"

The landlord eyed him suspiciously. "You're not a local policeman."

"I'm not a policeman at all," Joe retorted. "I'm a private investigator… sort of. Carl, if you don't answer me, you'll answer Inspector Perry. What were you talking about?"

As suspicious as his father, Carl shrugged. "He was looking for Darlene Garbutt."

"Was he now?"

Carl nodded. "I told him I didn't know where she lived, but he could find her at the wedding yesterday."

"You know Darlene, then?"

The landlord stepped in. "We know them all, Mr Murray. Wes, Kelly, Rott and Darlene. Known them for quite some time."

"Yes, well, Rott has been arrested for Pitman's murder."

Bernard's eyebrows rose, Carl looked uncomfortable and Joe latched onto it.

"How well do you know Darlene, Carl?"

The younger man shrugged. "Not well. She drinks in here now and then."

"Then why would Pitman ask you where to find her?"

Carl's ears coloured. "I, er, I dunno. He just pulled me and said, 'I'm looking for a woman named Darlene Garbutt. Do you know her?' I said I did and he asked me where I might find her."

"And you just sat down while you told him?"

Vetch intervened again. "You run a café, you said. You know what it's like when you're on your feet all day. You pinch five minutes when you can. And talking of being on your feet, we have customers to serve. Now if there's nothing else, Mr Murray…"

Vetch left his words hanging, and Joe nodded. "Thanks," he said, and made for the exit, followed closely by Maddy.

The sunshine at the front of the pub, hit Joe like a hammer. He glanced around for shade such as they had enjoyed in the beer garden and couldn't find any. He took out his tobacco.

"Are you all right?" Maddy asked.

He waved an irritable hand at the air. "Too hot. I'm hard up getting my breath."

She eyed the cigarette. "And that'll make it so much easier, won't it?"

Joe tutted and drew as deep a breath as he could. "Don't you start," he gasped. "I have enough of that from Sheila and Brenda."

"Sheila and Brenda?" Maddy asked. "Your wife and daughter?"

Joe laughed. "No fear. They're the friends I was telling you about. Only friends."

"Good friends, I'd say, if they're trying to stop you smoking," Maddy observed. "So, Joe, does all this bugger up your theories?"

"No. It's just another complication. A lot of what Carl said there makes sense, but there are bits which don't. The way he describes it, it's innocent. They way you describe it, it's as if Pitman know Carl Vetch. What I have to ask myself is, does it have any bearing on Pitman's death?"

"Well, I hope you sort it out, Joe, but I'd better get back to my graves. I'm due back in Cragshaven tomorrow afternoon."

"Maybe I'll see you around before then, huh?"

Maddy smiled generously. "You never know your luck in a big lake."

She offered her hand and Joe shook it.

"It's been fun, Maddy," he said, "and if you're ever in Sanford again, be sure to pop into the Lazy Luncheonette for a brew and a butty. I won't even charge you for the tea."

"Very gracious, I'm sure. Next time you're in Scarborough, be sure to look me up. And if there's any way I can ever help you, Joe, give me a shout."

Joe watched her amble away. "You can count on it."

As Maddy's figure disappeared into the crowds, Joe checked

his watch again and read 11:45. He made his way towards the boat station, queued up, bought his ticket, then joined a second queue waiting for the next boat to dock.

He leaned on a guard rail and looked out, north along the lakeshore. Forensic officers were working on a compact car on the car park. With absolutely no evidence to support the theory, Joe assumed it was Pitman's.

Beyond the car park, a narrow path led into the reeds and trees of the shoreline. It too was closed off by police, 'scene of crime' tape. A couple of hundred yards distant, Joe could see the dark shape of a roof, and he guessed it was the old boathouse.

While he waited, his mind tumbling on events, he lit his cigarette and suffered a bout of excruciating, uncontrollable coughing.

He glared at the cigarette as if it had somehow betrayed him. "They don't understand," he said to the smoke. "It isn't you. It's the heat."

# Chapter Nine

Joe was surprised by how long it did not take to get to Hilltop Farm. The water taxi took only a few minutes to cross from Bowness to the Ferry Landing on the other side, and once on the small bus, it took less than ten minutes to get to the farm.

After paying his admission fee, he worked his way quickly through the house and its exhibits celebrating the life and work of Beatrix Potter, including her writing desk, doll's house, and the many other pieces from which she drew her inspiration, and then made his way out into the gardens to seek out his companions.

He found Lee and Cheryl, entertaining their son on the children's trail, following the clues through the riot of summer flowers, which would help them solve the word puzzle. Danny was excited as ever, clutching his souvenirs, following his mother's prompts to take in the areas of special interest linked to the stories.

"I dunno where Aunty Sheila and Aunty Brenda have got to," Lee confessed. "I think they were looking for the ladies and then a brew."

"I'll catch up with them," Joe said taking out his wallet. He handed over a twenty. "Here. Spoil Danny a bit more."

"He's had enough spent on him, Uncle Joe," Cheryl protested.

"No. A kid like him, he can never have enough. Now do like I say and spend it on him."

Making for the exit, he rang Sheila.

"We're in the Tower Bank Arms," she said. "Behind Hilltop

Farm."

"I'll be there in two minutes," Joe promised. He made his way back down to the road, and turned sharp left to the pub.

A white-fronted building, retaining its bygone charm, like the Waterside in Bowness, both the bar and the dining room were packed with visitors. After obtaining drinks, he made his way back outside and found Sheila and Brenda at a wooden picnic table, sheltering from the sun under a parasol.

Sheila appeared relieved to see him but Brenda was as moody as she had been the previous night and earlier in the morning.

"You've been a long time, Joe," Sheila said. "What have you been up to?"

"The usual," he replied and sipped on his glass of lager. "Poking my nose in where it's not wanted."

He gave them a brief rundown of his conversation with Darlene, Maddy and Vetch.

"So where does all that leave you?" Sheila asked.

"In urgent need of a word with Perry," he replied.

"Anything in a skirt," Brenda grumbled.

Joe glared and was on the point of picking her up, when Sheila intervened again.

"It doesn't clear Paul's name, though, does it?"

"Rott?" Joe shook his head. "No, it doesn't, but it makes it less likely." He rolled a cigarette, lit it, and went through his usual coughing routine. Struggling to regain his breath, he gasped, "I need to know whether this drugs rumour is true."

"What difference will it make?"

He dragged again on the cigarette and this time, drawing the smoke into his lungs, held his breath for a few seconds. When he let it out, he was pleased to find that there was no accompanying cough.

"Just suppose that Pitman really was into drugs, and what Maddy saw was a meeting with one of his dealers? Carl Vetch. Maybe he owed Pitman money. Maybe there was a deal going down that Pitman didn't like or want. It could have turned nasty, and it could be the reason he was killed. Carl was decidedly edgy when I talked to him, and I get the impression he knew Darlene better than he was saying, and he may have known Pitman."

"Speculation, Joe," Sheila warned. "You have absolutely no proof."

"Neither have the police. Not against Rott, anyway." He glanced across the table at Brenda's sour face. "Have you anything to add, Brenda?"

She stood. "Yes. Why do we spend so much time worrying about other peoples' welfare and ignoring our own? Excuse me." She marched away from the table and back into the pub.

Joe stared after her. "What the hell was that about?"

"I don't know," Sheila replied. "At least, I don't think I know. Yesterday, I was certain it was wedding blues but now I'm not so sure."

"I'm not sure I can take much more of this, Sheila. Two more words out of her and I swear I will snap."

"Leave it with me, Joe. I'll have a word."

By one o'clock they were back on the boat to Windermere. Sheila and Brenda sat at the rear, deep in conversation. Joe, Lee, Cheryl and Danny were at the front, Joe indulging his great-nephew pointing out the highlights on the lake, the boats and yachts, the birds and describing other wildlife which the banks might harbour.

Once back on the eastern shore, Lee and Cheryl made their way to the hotel with a tired Danny, while Joe, Sheila and Brenda caught a local bus into the centre of Windermere, where the women could indulge in more shopping, and Joe could ruminate on the many possibilities swimming around his head.

While the two women made their way round the narrow, elongated loop of Crescent Road and Main Road, Joe noticed that Brenda purposely avoided him. He dismissed it as womanly moodiness. Whatever was wrong with her would no doubt come out sometime in the near future, and he was certain it was nothing to do with him.

Stepping out of a newsagent on Main Road, grateful for the shade provided by the old, dark stone buildings on both sides of the road, he was surprised to bump into Rott.

"They let you go, then?"

He nodded. "I kept telling 'em I was innocent, Mr Murray," he said.

Joe spotted the bunch of flowers in Rott's hand. "Peace offering?"

The younger man blushed and nodded. "For Darlene. We were gonna... well, you know. Last night. Plod put the mockers on that, though."

Joe looked around and indicated The Tarnside Tea Room. "Come on. Let's get a cuppa. I wanna talk to you."

"Yeah, but—"

"Never mind the yeah, buts. Get in here."

Ushering Rott through the door, he rang Sheila to let her know where to find them, then settled into a table by the window and waited for service.

The waitress, a trim, dark-haired woman of about twenty-five, gave Rott a familiar nod and smile when she took their order.

The gesture was not lost on Joe. "You're well known round here, Rott?"

He smiled shyly. "You know how it is, Mr Murray."

"For God's sake call me Joe."

Rott shrugged, and gazed through the windows at a shop across the road. Joe followed his gaze. The place displayed memorabilia of the Lake District, and had garnered a small crowd at the window.

"Me and Wes, we came here working the summer season on a caravan park t'other side of Ambleside," Rott went on. "We liked it that much, we decided to set up here. Let's face it, it's better than Sanford, innit?"

"I happen to like Sanford," Joe argued, "but I can see where you're coming from. Go on."

"There's a skill shortage in this country, you know. We were lucky. My dad and Wes's insisted that we learned a trade. We both had a few bob in the bank, my old man lent me some money, Alec shoved Wes a few thou, and we were in business. We've never really looked back. We take on any kinda work, you know. I do the electrics, Wes is licensed for the gas as well as water, and if we get bigger jobs, like a bitta roofing or bricklaying, we sub the work out. Didn't take us long to get a reputation." Rott smiled at the waitress as she brought their tea. "And it weren't only for our work."

Joe chuckled. "Pair of jack the lads, eh? I was at the Waterside earlier. The landlord there knows you, too."

"Bernie Vetch? Tight-fisted old git, he is. Screw the price down to the last ha'penny." Rott laughed. "Generous with the free beer when you're working there, mind."

"I'm generous with the free tea when people work in my place," Joe said, logging the information about Vetch into his brain. "All right, Rott, so you're well known. Now tell me what happened yesterday."

The big man frowned. "I don't know cos I can't remember."

"You'd had a fair bit to drink," Joe prompted him.

"To be honest, I didn't think I had. A coupla glasses of bubbly, sure, but that's baby water, innit? I know I was well tanked up when he came in shouting the odds at Darlene, but I don't know why."

Joe let it go and changed tack. "What did Pitman say to rile you so much?"

"He threatened Darlene. Told her if she didn't stop sending him texts, he'd shut her up for good. I just lost it." Rott smiled wanly. "You know me."

"I know you have tunnel vision when you get into a fight. You just land out at anyone."

Joe stared through the window again. Sheila and Brenda were now in front of the souvenir shop, pointing and chattering, and he could imagine Sheila saying, 'Oh, that would look lovely in my tallboy'.

Brenda appeared to be her usual self with Sheila: chatty and cheerful, and it caused Joe to wonder if it really was him she was mad at. They had had a brief fling ever since February, but it had petered out to nothing over the last month or two. Brenda appeared untroubled about it, and it was no big deal for Joe. They had never intended it to be serious.

The thought prompted him again. "You and Darlene. What's the score between you two? Serious?"

Rott considered the question. "Well, I wouldn't have said that. We've been seeing quite a bit of one another, and we spend nights at my place, but we're not planning on getting wed or owt. I mean, to be honest with you, she's been round the block a time or two since she got here. Jumped every bloke in the Waterside except for Bernard Vetch and that poof, Storm. She was steady with Carl Vetch for months, at one bit."

Again logging the information into his mind, Joe hid his surprise and said, "I didn't know Storm was like that."

"I don't know, either, "Rott replied, "but Darlene wasn't interested in him. Wrong star sign or summat."

Joe laughed. "People take that guff seriously?"

Rott nodded. "Darlene does. Storm's a Libra so it's a non-starter according to what she told me. I'm a Capricorn so I'm better with her."

Joe struggled to suppress his humour. "And what's Darlene?"

"Virgo."

There was a moment's silence and they both laughed.

Sobering up, Joe asked, "What about her brothers?"

"Well I'm not getting down to it with them, am I?" Rott laughed and drank some tea. "No, I never met them until they turned up the day before yesterday. Not bad lads, Joe."

"They looked bad enough when they were showing Pitman the way out."

"They were just narked. See, Darlene says Pitman was the reason she left London and came up here. He was hounding her. And she's been getting regular texts from him since she got here."

"Yeah, she told me."

"Well, they're her brothers, aren't they?" Rott declared. "Bound to want to look after their little sister."

Joe, too, drank tea, and glanced across the street. Sheila and Brenda had gone into the shop by now.

Bringing his attention back to the business at hand, he asked, "Any idea how Pitman came to be here, Rott?"

"Haven't the foggiest."

Joe put the question to one side. "Listen, lad, I don't want all the gory details, but what happened with you and Darlene yesterday afternoon, when you left the reception?"

Rott's features fell. "Not a lot. I was really smashed by then. We went back to the room and she was feeling a bit, er, frisky, if you know what I mean. I hit the bed, and the next thing I remember I was waking up and it was nearly seven o'clock. And Darlene was in a right mood."

Joe's companions emerged from the shop across the street. Both had small carrier bags. Sheila was peering into hers, Brenda talking to her. Sheila looked up and across the street. The two women exchanged a few more words, then crossed the street and entered the Tarnside.

"Hello, Joe, hello Paul," Sheila greeted them.

Brenda contented herself with a nod, and took the seat next to Rott, on the other side of the table from Joe, while Sheila took the remaining seat alongside their boss.

"How are you, Paul?" Brenda asked.

"I'm all right, thanks, Mrs Jump. All things considered."

Joe waited for Brenda to ask about him. When she did not, he opened his mouth to challenge her, but the waitress arrived

103

and took an order from Sheila for two cream teas.

"We've bought you a little something, Joe," Sheila said and reached into her carrier bag.

She handed over a boxed model of a chef. Joe took it out and studied it. About four inches high, with his chef's hat pulled over his eyes, he held a butcher's chopper in one hand. It stood on a small plinth along which was printed the message, *Whaddya want?*

Sheila tittered at Joe's surprise. "We could have the message personalised and we thought that fitted you."

"Very funny." Joe put it back in the box and handed it back. "I'll put it on the shelf with the beakers in the Lazy Luncheonette." He turned to Brenda. "Now listen—"

He was interrupted again by the waitress bringing the food and drink for the two women.

"So, Paul," Brenda asked, deliberately (so it appeared to Joe) ignoring the angry glances coming her way, "have the police officially cleared you?"

Rott shook his head. "They haven't got anything to hold me on, but they warned me they might need to speak to me again, so I can't leave the area." His voice changed, the tones almost pleading. "Honestly, it weren't me. If I could have got me hands on him, I might have smacked him about a bit, but I wouldn't have killed him. Not even by accident."

Sheila swallowed a mouthful of scone and wiped cream from her fingers."You had had a lot to drink, Paul."

"That's just it, Mrs Riley. I was telling Mr Murray, I hadn't. All I had were a couple of glasses of champagne."

"Potent stuff, that shampoo," Brenda said. "Ask misery guts over there. He knows. Anything stronger than brown ale and he's blathered after two sniffs."

Joe was stung into retaliation. "I've had enough of this. Brenda, if you've got something to say to me, get it said, and cut out this bloody sniping and cold shouldering."

"I have nothing to say to you."

"Then get the pole out of your arse."

Joe had inadvertently raised his voice, and seconds later, the waitress was at their table. Keeping her voice low, she said, "I'm sorry, sir, but could you keep the noise down, please. We do have other customers to consider."

Joe huffed out his breath. "Sorry. Yes. Of course." The waitress wandered off and Joe glowered at Brenda. "Now look what you've done."

Brenda opened her mouth to answer, but Sheila, speaking to Rott, headed off the inevitable argument.

"Could someone have put something in your drink?"

Rott reacted as if he did not understand the question, but Joe's face lit up.

"Damn right they could," he said.

"But why?" Rott cried. "Some kinda sick joke?"

"Nope," Joe replied. "It's one way of ensuring that you couldn't account for your movements."

"But Darlene could tell 'em."

"Not if her drink had been spiked too." Joe drank his tea. "Listen, Rott, what are you doing tonight? Going home?"

"Nah. We're staying at the Lakeside Manor. Off home tomorrow."

"The minute Minnie and Moanie here have finished their snack, we'd better get back there. I have to speak to Inspector Perry, and you'd better be prepared to give them a sample."

"It'll be too late, surely?" Sheila said.

"Depends what was used," Joe ventured. "Some drugs can hang about in your system for anything up to forty-eight hours. They may still get a trace." He pondered the situation for a moment. "One last thing, Rott. The overalls they found near the body."

Rott's face fell. "Mine."

"Definitely?"

"Definitely." He patted his expanded belly. "I'm bigger than Wes."

"And if you killed him then left your overalls there, you're stupider than Lee."

"Or stupider than him," Brenda grumbled with a finger point at Joe.

He was about to respond when a warning glance from Sheila stopped him. He lapsed into silence for a moment, partly to let his temper cool down, partly to consider Rott's overalls.

"How difficult would it be for someone to get hold of your overalls?"

"Not easy," Rott admitted. "I keep 'em in the van because I don't always wear them."

Sheila tutted. "What happened to health and safety, Paul?"

"All right for the town hall wallahs to whine about, Mrs Riley, but not when you're at the sharp end. See, if we're working in someone's house, they don't want dirty overalls dragging everywhere, so I get by with jeans and T's. I only use the overalls on really dirty jobs. But the van's kept locked up all the time."

Joe had his doubts. "All the time?"

"Tools and stuff in it, Mr Murray. All the time."

"In that case, someone has gone to a great deal of trouble to pin this on you, and the only way we can clear your name is to find out who."

# Chapter Ten

It was after three by the time they got back to the Lakeside Manor. Sheila and Brenda retired to their room and Joe rang Perry asking to see her ASAP, and she agreed to meet him on the lawns at three thirty.

Sheila joined him a few minutes before, and announced, "Brenda is sleeping it off," she announced.

"Have you found out what's wrong with her?" Joe demanded.

Sheila eyed the car park where Perry had just climbed out of her car. "Later."

Looking efficient, smart and yet cool in a dark grey business suit and white blouse, Perry joined them, and Joe ordered tea for them.

"It's been a busy day, and we've made quite a bit of progress," the inspector reported. "But I'll tell you about that in a little while. You asked to see me."

"Hmm, yes," Joe said as he rolled a cigarette. "We bumped into Rott in town earlier and he told us you'd let him go for the time being."

"We haven't enough evidence to continue holding him. However, he can't leave the area."

"And Darlene and her brothers?"

"To be frank, Joe, we have absolutely no evidence to link any of them to the crime."

Joe lit the cigarette and experienced another coughing fit under Perry's watchful eye.

"Have you ever heard of COPD, Joe?" she asked.

He shook his head and drew as deep a breath as he could. "Some kind of police organisation, is it? Like Scientific Support?"

"No. It's Chronic Obstructive Pulmonary Disease; the modern name for emphysema. A lot of heavy smokers suffer from it. I'm no doctor, but you should get your breathing checked because you may be one of them."

"Pah. Rubbish." He coughed again. "Hot weather, that's what it is. I'm a moderate smoker."

"You roll your own," Perry observed. "It's difficult to keep track of the number of cigarettes you smoke."

"I also work in catering, and I can't smoke indoors. We're so busy, I don't get time for a smoke."

"So he makes time," Sheila said. "Joe, Brenda and I have been telling you for years you need to stop."

"Never mind my smoking," he grumbled, and aimed his beady glance at Perry. "I said we'd bumped into Rott in town, and we had a bit of a natter about yesterday. He has no memory of the afternoon. He got back to his room, his head hit the pillow, and he was gone."

"Yes, I know. He told us he was totally plastered."

"Did you bother to ask how much he had drunk?" Joe demanded.

Perry blushed. "Er, no, quite honestly. We just assumed that as it was a wedding, he would have had a lot."

"Not so," Joe said, and took another drag on the cigarette. After his coughing had subsided, he said, "He told us he'd had no more than two glasses of bubbly."

"We think, Inspector, that someone may have put something in his drink."

"Ah. I see." Perry took out her phone and spent a few minutes barking orders into it. At length she shut off the phone. "If someone put Drummond out, he would have no alibi, especially if Darlene was out, too. I've ordered one of our Scientific Support people to turn up here and take a urine sample. It's only just twenty-four hours. If there was anything in his drink, it will show up. But it seems to me it would be necessary to knock Darlene out, too."

"We figured that," Joe agreed. "I spoke to Darlene this morning, before we went hunting Jemima Puddleduck and Squirrel bloody Nutkin. She and Rott tell the same story. They were on a promise yesterday afternoon, and yet he got blathered before they went back to the room. I know he can be a bit of a banana, especially when he loses his rag, but he's not totally dumb. If he knew he was gonna get his legover, he'd have eased off the sauce, not taken more on board."

"The only one who might gain an advantage from that is Darlene Garbutt. She could take the opportunity to sneak out while he was still asleep, kill Pitman and get back before he woke, and yet we're sure she didn't."

"She also admits she was out of it for most of the afternoon. See, they're providing the alibi for each other. If both of them were asleep all afternoon, both alibis are shot. If it was a third party, say someone at the reception, then they could have actually done the job knowing that you would look at Rott and then Darlene." Joe frowned as Perry's words finally registered. "You're sure she didn't? How come?"

"I told you last night. Pitman was already dead, or very nearly, when he was hanged. How would a frail thing like Darlene lift him up to slip the camera strap over the hook? I don't think she's tall enough for one thing. Do you know where she is?"

Both Joe and Sheila shook their heads.

"We haven't seen her since this morning," Joe replied. "We've been doing quite a bit of asking round."

The waiter returned with their tea, and there was a delay while Sheila poured for them.

When they were all settled with refreshments, Joe asked, "Have you spoken to the landlord at the Waterside?"

"Bernard Vetch? Yes," Perry said. "And he told us Pitman

and his son, Carl, had a chat last night, when Pitman asked about Darlene Garbutt. We don't think it's significant, other than it tells us Pitman came here looking for her. "

"I'm gonna reserve judgement on that for a minute." Joe sipped his tea and took a satisfying drag on his cigarette. "I was speaking to another guest from the Waterside earlier. Madeleine Chester."

Perry nodded. "We have a statement from her. Not that she could tell us much."

"That's the difference between formal questioning and chitchat," Joe said with a smile. "You get the facts, I get information. Gossip in the Waterside has it that you found drugs in Pitman's room."

Perry clucked impatiently and put down her cup and saucer. "Chinese bloody whispers. There are times when I hate this job. By the time it makes Monday morning's tabloids, you'll find that the pub has been staging a convention for international drug cartels."

"So there's no truth in it?" Sheila asked.

"We found traces of cocaine in Pitman's bags," the inspector admitted. "It could indicate he was carrying more, but if so, we haven't found any. On the other hand, it could indicate that he was a user and he'd disposed of a wrap on Thursday night. We don't know. As matters stand, we do not know that the murder is drug related, and we are working on the theory that it was something to do with the argument at the wedding yesterday afternoon."

Something in her tone called to Joe. "There's something you're not telling us."

The inspector nodded. "We had frogmen in the lake this morning. They've found what we believe is the murder weapon. Forensic have it right now. No blood, obviously, but there may still be traces of hair and perhaps microscopic traces of skin still attached to it, even though it's been in the water overnight."

"Where it could have been for months," Joe objected.

Perry shook her head. "It's not rusted. Well greased, you see. Something that has been in continuous use." She paused a moment. "It's a Stillson wrench. Do you know what that is?"

Sheila looked blank, but Joe knew. "Heavy duty adjustable pipe wrench. Plumbers use them…" He gaped at Perry. "Not Wes Staines."

"We're not sure, but we think so. It has the letter 'W' scratched into it on the handle. Wes would certainly have one in his toolbox. Anyone who works with pipes would carry one."

Sheila glanced at her watch. "He'll be landing in the Maldives about now."

"According to my calculations, Mrs Riley, it'll be half past seven this evening before they get there. The flight is about eleven hours, not eight."

"No, I'm not having this," Joe said. "Even if the wrench does belong to Wes, you don't know that it's the murder weapon, and if it is, that doesn't mean Wes was the one who used it. If it was in his van, for instance, anyone could have nicked it at any time."

"All of that is perfectly true, Joe, which is why I don't regret letting Wes and Kelly go off on honeymoon. However, he does have some questions to answer. I've spoken with a senior police officer in Malé and they'll intercept him as he gets off the plane. I've arranged a video call with Mr Staines for later tonight, when he gets there. By then, I'm hoping forensic can tell us something."

"His car is on the car park, here," Sheila pointed out. "One of those four by fours. If it was in the back, it could have been stolen yesterday."

"The alarm would have trigged, and it hasn't," Joe said. "He'd more likely keep it in his van, but like Rott's overalls, you then have to account for someone taking both. Inspector, what are the chances of this *not* being the murder weapon?"

"According to our pathologist, very slim. The skull indentation and surrounding damage are consistent with something of this nature. We'll know more, later. For now, we have another problem. Mr Pitman's camera or cameras. We can't find it or them."

"He was using what looked like a Canon 650 when I saw him yesterday," Joe announced. He smiled at Perry's surprise. "I have an old Sony DSLR, and I was a bit envious. Mind, he was a pro, so he would need the top range tackle, wouldn't he?"

"A very expensive piece of tackle, Joe," Perry agreed. "So where is it? When we found him his bag was nearby, and it contains the usual equipment: lenses, external flash guns, batteries, even some rolls of film. His body was hanged with the strap. But the camera was missing. And it's safe to assume it will not have been the only camera he had on him. These people usual carry a digital compact."

"You've checked his vehicle, I take it?" Sheila asked.

Perry nodded. "And his hotel room. The only thing in the room was his overnight bag. That's where we found the drug traces. Amongst his clothing. His car was found on the public car park at the boat station, but there was no sign of the camera or cameras in there, either."

"That must be the one we saw the police going through when we caught the boat back from Sawrey," Joe ventured.

"It'll be towed away shortly," Perry said. "We think he drove to the boat station from here when the Garbutt brothers chased him off yesterday." She concentrated on Joe. "Have you learned anything else?"

"Not really."

"Then we have to take a closer look at everyone invited to the wedding to see how many of them may have a connection to Pitman." She laid a steely eye on Joe. "Right now, the finger is pointing at Wes Staines as much as anyone. His wife posed for Pitman, remember. We have only Wes's word that he learned of that last night."

Sheila's eyes widened. "Kelly did what?"

Joe clucked. "Damn. I'm sorry, Sheila, but you didn't know, did you?" he went on to tell her of Kelly's history with Pitman. "Mum's the word," he concluded. "That's girl's future rests on absolute secrecy."

Her lips pursed in disapproval, Sheila said, "Well that explains quite a lot, but if young Wes was putting on an act, he's a different Wes to the one we knew," Sheila said. "He was never that good a liar."

"People change, Mrs Riley."

"There's another thing," Joe said. "If the killer was from this hotel, he may be on CCTV."

"We have that to check, Joe," Perry admitted, "and of course, we'll get to it, but it doesn't necessarily follow. If we assume that Wes or Paul Drummond carried out the killing, it could have been set up days ago. We will check on it."

Joe nodded. "That applies if it was anyone. They don't have to have been staying at this hotel. And that means you have to look at the victim. Have you done your homework on Pitman yet?"

"I have officers tracking him down, but it takes a day or two to get a full picture. We haven't yet found a mobile phone, either. You'd be surprised what we can learn from them."

"It was something I meant to ask," Joe said. "I spoke to Darlene Garbutt this morning, and she tells me that Pitman kept texting her, hassling her, but she dumped all the messages. If that was so, they'd show up on his mobile, too, wouldn't they?"

"Unless he had erased them," Perry admitted. "In which case, we can still get the records from his mobile company. We know he had one. We found business cards in his bag with the number on. We're tracking down the company and we'll be accessing his records the moment we can. Darlene's too."

"What about the shed where he was found?" Sheila asked.

"It's just along the lake from the boat station, isn't it? Have you checked the CCTV from the boat station?"

"Again we're on with it, Mrs Riley, but it's a slow, painstaking process. There are hours of footage to be viewed, and even then, there are no guarantees that either Pitman or his killer were caught on camera." Perry sighed. "A cursory check on Pitman has revealed he was a bit of a sleaze merchant. His website advertises wedding services, portraits, and he took commissions for things like landscapes, but the major part of his work was, er, glamour, for want of a better description."

"You mean skin," Joe said and Perry nodded.

"He sold to lowbrow soft porn magazines, supplied pictures for those kinds of websites, and he offered low cost glamour portfolios for wannabe models. He didn't have a good reputation amongst his peers."

"I'll read up on him when I get back to my room," Joe promised.

"Good. Now come on, Joe, you know everything? What's this you said you were reserving judgement on?"

"When I spoke to Darlene, I asked if there were any boyfriends who might have been peeved after they finished. Someone who might have got in touch with Pitman and told him where she was, or sent him her mobile number. She said there weren't. She'd had a few boyfriends, but nothing serious. Rott told me that she was going steady with Carl Vetch for some time. Maddy Chester told me when she saw Pitman and Carl talking last night, Carl sat down for a while, and it was a serious conversation. To me that suggests two men who either knew each other or had business to discuss, and Carl was very hazy on it when I spoke to him."

"Hmm. All right. What of it?" Perry asked.

"Suppose Carl was seriously teed off when they finished? Suppose he called Pitman to get him up here. Let's suppose something else. Vetch left his pub in the hands of others yesterday while he supervised a catering do at the Lakeside Manor. Odd thing to do, that. Suppose he wanted to be at the wedding because he knew Pitman was going to be there, and suppose that confrontation with Darlene was a front for something else." Joe stared at Perry. "Like a big deal going down."

"And something went wrong in the old boathouse," Perry concluded.

Joe nodded and she considered it.

"How would Vetch get hold of Paul Drummond's overalls?"

"Rott told me Vetch was generous with the free beer for workmen. Obviously, he's worked at that pub at some time."

"Recently?"

"You'd have to ask Rott," Joe said.

"The only problem I can see, Joe, is that it would mean Pitman was lured up here specifically to kill him and then frame Paul Drummond and/or Wes Staines, Darlene, Kelly and so on."

"And that is exactly what I'm thinking," Joe declared.

"Interesting idea and I'll give it some thought," Perry said. "Vetch is known for some of his, er, fiddles, shall we say. A little too much water in the whisky bottle, cash transactions with the draymen. You know the kind of thing I mean."

He certainly does when it comes to the draymen," Sheila chuckled.

Perry smiled and looked at her watch. "Like I said, I'll think about it. For now, if you'll excuse me, I have a life to lead other than sitting on this lawn chatting to you. You will keep me posted on anything you turn up, won't you?"

"Sure," Joe agreed. "And you'll keep us up to date on your progress."

"You have my word on it."

"Any chance I can sit in on this video conference with Wes?"

Perry hesitated a moment, then made her mind. "Yes. You

115

know him, and he may feel more relaxed with you at this end, so I don't see why not. Come along to the station about half past seven." With a nod she turned and walked away.

"Pleasant woman," Sheila observed, watching Perry make her way back into the hotel.

"Hard as nails," Joe disagreed. "Like all cops."

"Like a certain someone we know who is not a police officer."

Joe frowned and rolled another cigarette. "What is wrong with her, Sheila? Has she told you?"

"Not in so many words, but I think I know, and you should know, too." Sheila laid a stern eye on him. "Think back to a conversation you and I had in a café in Weston-super-Mare earlier in the year."

"Oh, that." He stuck the completed cigarette in his mouth. Digging into the pockets of his gilet, he said, "Brenda and me haven't been, er, an item for a few weeks now. Nothing wrong, but I told you at Easter it was never going to go anywhere." He took out his Zippo and lit the cigarette. A nasty bout of coughing followed. When he was through it, still wheezing, he grumbled, "I wish this damned weather would cool off."

Sheila tutted. "Joe, promise me something. When we get back to Sanford, you'll go to the doctor's and have your chest checked."

"Sheila—"

"No, listen to me, Joe. I know those thing are causing the damage." She pointed at his cigarette. "But I could be wrong. You may have some kind of chest infection, and God forbid that it should be anything more serious, but you need to get it seen to. Now please, go to the doctor."

"All right, all right. If it makes you happy, I'll book an appointment. Now what about Brenda?"

Sheila let her hands flop into her lap. "I'm her best friend, and normally she tells me everything. She's been like it for days, now, Joe, and she's said nothing out loud, but I know

116

what it is… or I think I know. And it does hark back to that conversation in Weston-super-Mare, but you and her were not the only thing we talked about."

Still mystified, Joe said, "Yeah, well, I'm a big boy and I can take care of myself, but something is going to snap somewhere, so we're gonna have to sort it out." He stared across the lawns to the lake beyond. "What price Pitman's camera or cameras are at the bottom of that lake?"

The change of subject took Sheila by surprise, and she, too, looked to the water and the crowds enjoying the late afternoon sunshine. "Why do you say that?"

"Pitman was a photographer," Joe said. "What do photographers, especially professional ones, do? They take pictures."

She frowned. "I don't understand, Joe."

"Ask yourself a question. What was Pitman doing in that old shed?"

Still watching the boats on the lake, their wakes criss-crossing the water, Sheila remained silent for a moment, then turned to meet Joe's eyes. "He was waiting to meet his killer."

"That's my guess, too, only he didn't know he was going to his death. Now, suppose he got there a few minutes ahead of the arranged meeting time, what would he do?" Joe hastened to answer his own question. "He'd take pictures. Photographers do. They call it stock footage in the movie business. You take photos of an old shed and the surrounding area because you never know when you may be able to sell such a picture."

"Ah, right. I see what you mean. And he may have taken a picture of his killer."

Joe nodded and pulled on his cigarette again. "If the killer was already there, Pitman may have taken a picture as he walked into the shed. If he got there first, he may have taken a picture of the killer as he approached the shed. Either way, five'll get you ten, that there was an image of the killer on that camera, and the murderer dumped it in the lake along with the murder weapon. Even if the camera is found, the memory card will be ruined. The cops would never get anything from it."

# Chapter Eleven

After calling at reception to book dinner for six thirty instead of the usual seven thirty, Joe returned to his room, plugged in his netbook, and once it was up and running, he Googled *Adam Pitman Photographer* and the first result took him to Pitman's website.

He was not impressed.

To begin with the site was hosted on a free set up, and it looked home made. Joe, with help from Sheila and Brenda, had built websites for both the Lazy Luncheonette and the Sanford 3rd Age Club, but he had valid reasons for doing so. The Lazy Luncheonette did not need a significant web presence, and the 3rd Age Club was run for the benefit of its members, so needed a careful eye on sundry expenses. Neither site needed to be professional.

Pitman, on the other hand, was a man who plied his trade with visual media. Theoretically, he understood the value of professional presentation. Why, then, skimp on the cost of a website and hosting? Websites could be professionally built for a few hundred pounds, and Joe knew from experience that domain names and hosting could be had for less than £50 a year.

Delving further into the several dozen pages, his opinion of Pitman took a serious dip. The photographer offered family and business packages, but gave no indication of prices. He also offered portfolios for wannabe models, but again he gave no hint of his charges.

Joe eventually arrived at the gallery pages. There were some landscapes, mostly from the London area, including an impressive and spectacular, time-lapse image of the London Eye, the carriages of the famous wheel blurred as they crawled along. There were formal sittings of babies and children, brides and grooms, and then there were the 'glamour' shots.

Joe found nude modelling boring rather than distasteful, but when he saw the shots Pitman had produced, he turned that opinion on its head. Skin, he had said to Perry, and he revised that opinion downward, too. They were quite simply soft porn, soft because they involved women only, mostly in provocative, supposedly erotic, poses. Had there been a man in any of the pictures, they would have been classified as hardcore. The focus on every image was sexual. By the time he had skimmed through several hundred such images, each offering reprint rights, Joe felt a deep-seated disgust for both the man and his work.

He did, however, come away able to put Kelly's mind at rest. He wasn't sure how long ago she had posed for Pitman, but her face did not appear anywhere in the gallery.

He did however find a whole series of about thirty shots of Darlene. Some were obviously done in a studio and judging by the ordinariness of the furnishings, he guessed it was Pitman's (or Darlene's) home. Many others were done on location. He recognised the Cerne Abbas Giant instantly (who wouldn't?) and the base of the Angel of the North. There were pictures taken in a dilapidated old shed, which looked like it might have been a workshop at one time, several under a seaside pier, more in a beer garden, some in front of a stone-built pub, others with a fairground as a backdrop.

The only consistent aspect of the images was Darlene, and the only consistent thing about her was her lack of clothing.

Joe sat back and considered the implications of the gallery. He was not interested in Darlene's propensity for taking off her clothes. She, herself, admitted she had grown tired of that. It was the locations. Cerne Abbas was in the south of England, the Angel of the North was on Tyneside. Joe wasn't sure, but he estimated 400 miles separated the two locations, and the Angel of the North would be a good three hundred miles from London.

Pitman, then, was obviously not short of money, and yet, judging from the website, he didn't make it with his photography. So how?

The answer, dark and dangerous, occurred to him right away.

He was about to return to his basic search to follow up his theory, when he noticed the time coming up to 5.45pm. Shutting down the computer, he showered, changed, and made his way down to reception, where he ordered a taxi for seven fifteen, then moved to the dining room where he sat alone, chewed his way through an unspectacular cold meat salad, before taking a table on the lawns for a smoke and a beer.

He was joined almost immediately by Alec and Julia Staines, and Julia looked almost as angry as she had the previous night.

"They're interviewing Wes again," she snapped.

Coughing after lighting his cigarette, Joe shook his head at her, and when he had his breath back, said, "I'm not gonna do this with you, Julia. A man's been murdered, Wes and Rott are in the frame. Perry let Wes go to Malé, but it doesn't end there. Until he's officially cleared, they'll continue to question him."

"I'm not blaming you, Joe—"

"Well, you could have fooled me last night."

Julia drew breath as if trying to calm down. "All right, all right, I was wrong. You were trying your best, but you know Wes. He wouldn't do anything like this."

Joe blew out another stream of smoke. "Correction. I *knew* Wes. He's not the kid who used to come home with our Lee. And if you want my opinion, Pitman got exactly what he deserved, but it's still against the law and Wes has to be questioned." He switched his focus to Alec. "Have you been told about the pipe wrench?"

Alec nodded. "Perry showed it to us, but we can't say whether or not it's Wes's."

"There you go," Joe said. "The only person likely to know is Wes."

"You're sitting in on the session," Alec said.

"Yes. They figure a friendly face may make Wes more open." He took another drag on his cigarette. "I don't believe Wes is guilty. I don't think he had anything to do with it, and I don't think it's about Kelly. I've been making some inquiries today, and even though Perry won't have it, everything points to a meeting between Pitman and an unidentified man on Thursday night, so I'm more interested in what Kelly may be able to tell me, not Wes. Julia, you have to deal with this, and there's no point blaming me. Take your temper out on me if you must. I deal with bolshie truckers every day of my working life. I have a broad back and I can deal with you having a pop at me. I may cross you off my Christmas card list, but it won't alter the situation one iota."

Julia sulked quietly, but her husband remained more practical. "What do we do to prove him innocent, Joe?"

"There's nothing you can do. Listen to me, Alec; the cops have no proof against Wes, Rott or anyone else. They have questions, and Wes has to answer those questions. If he can satisfy them that the murder weapon is not his, or if it is, that he didn't hit Pitman with it, then they'll leave him alone. Right now, it looks a bit grim. The wrench as Perry explained it to me, is fairly new, well looked after. It has a letter W scratched into the handle. That might make it Wes's, it might not. If it is his, he'll have to account for how it came to hit Pitman on the head… or should I say, he'll have to account for how someone else got hold of it to hit Pitman on the head. But even if he can't explain that, it doesn't mean he'll be arrested. It's only one strand of the investigation. He has a motive—" Joe clammed up, realising he had said too much already.

Tight-lipped, Julia said, "You mean because Kelly posed for Pitman?"

"Ah. So you know?"

"Wes and Kelly told us about it on the way to the airport this morning, Joe," Alec said.

"But he didn't know about it," Julia protested. "Not until she told him last night."

"He says he didn't know," Joe corrected her, "and I believe him. The police are less biased than me or you." Joe checked his watch. "Now, if you'll excuse me, I have to get out front to meet the taxi."

Alec nodded. "Good on you, Joe. We'll be in the bar later if you want to bring us up to date."

"You have my word on it."

From the lawns, Joe passed into the Beatrix Potter room where he found Sheila and Brenda waiting to be called for dinner. He had a brief word with Sheila, and since Brenda all but ignored him, he did likewise, and left through reception, where he paused to speak with Harriet Atkinson.

Going on the defensive before Joe could even speak, she announced, "Your taxi hasn't arrived yet, Mr Murray."

"That's okay. I needed a word anyway."

With the look of a headmistress suspecting impertinence in a fourth former, she asked, "A word?"

"You don't like overalls, do you?" Joe asked.

"I think overalls are necessary, Mr Murray, for people who do dirty or manual jobs. I do not like to see them in reception." She glared. "Any more than I like to see a guest dressed in shabby shorts."

Joe ignored the jibe. "So nobody could have got in or out through reception yesterday wearing a pair of overalls?"

"Not while I was on duty." There was no doubt in Mrs

Atkinson's voice. "And Mr Nelson is just as strict."

"And they couldn't have sneaked into the Beatrix Potter room, then out across the lawns?"

She was less certain this time. "That may just be possible, but we had staff working outside yesterday, and I know my staff. If they saw anyone in overalls crossing the lawns, they would have reported the matter. If not the staff, then I'm certain one of the guests would have raised an eyebrow."

"Good, good. I like to see standards maintained. Except when they apply to me." Joe grinned at her obvious irritation. "Now think about this. Could someone have carried the overalls out in a large plastic bag; a bin liner for example."

"Well, of course they could. They could also have brought the overalls in amongst their luggage."

Joe shook his head. "No one in his right mind would carry a pair of overalls in a suitcase full of clean clothing."

"They could if they were in a bin liner."

Joe disagreed. "Even in a bin liner, I wouldn't do it. I'm not the best dressed man in town … you've probably noticed … but I would never do that." He chewed over his thoughts for a moment. "Have the police checked your CCTV yet?"

"I'm not sure I should tell you."

He tutted. "For God's sake, woman, I'm on my way to the police station to help them question the bride and groom."

"Oh." Mrs Atkinson was taken aback by the announcement and Joe guessed she felt he shouldn't be allowed to question a motorist parking illegally. "In that case, yes. They've taken copies of the recordings."

"Thanks. I'll wait outside for the taxi."

The sun would not set for another two hours, but at this time on the car park, it was behind the hotel and the building cast a cool shadow where Joe could wait. Lighting a cigarette, he allowed the coughing fit to expire, and then engaged his agile brain on the problems before him: the murder of Adam Pitman and the mood of Brenda Jump.

Of the two, Brenda's mood was far and away the more intractable. The murder of Pitman could be explained in any number of ways, but the information was, as yet, incomplete. Where Brenda was concerned, the information was not so much incomplete as non-existent.

As was the case with Sheila, he had known Brenda since childhood when they all attended the same primary and secondary schools. Jovial and fun loving most of the time, she could be fiery and temperamental when she chose, but it was rare that she sulked the way she had done for the last day or two.

Sheila had hinted that a clue lay in a conversation in the café of Weston-super-Mare's Winter Gardens. Joe recalled the conversation well. Brenda had gone off to buy Easter eggs for charity, leaving Joe and Sheila to enjoy a cup of coffee and a heart to heart on the casual relationship between Joe and Brenda. Sheila's concern lay in the effect it may have on their working relationship, and Joe had largely pooh-poohed the idea. Neither he nor Brenda had seen it as anything other than the occasional night spent together. Brenda was well-known for such dates and Joe had always said he was in no hurry for another permanent relationship.

They had gone on to talk about Joe's marriage and Sheila and Brenda's widowhood, and their different approaches to the single life. Sheila had shown no interest in other men, Brenda had taken the opposite route while Joe had maintained what he considered to be a healthy cynicism with regard to marriage, all of which came as a result of the way their marriages had ended. Alison walked out on Joe, Peter Riley had been killed by two heart attacks coming close together, and Colin Jump had died of cancer.

But even though he could recall the conversation, Joe could not see any hint to Brenda's behaviour right now. Unless it was something to do with Colin, but if so, it had taken the better part of five or six years to show through.

The toot of a horn brought him back to the here and now, sat on a bench outside The Lakeside Manor Hotel, enjoying a cigarette in the evening shade.

A four-year-old black Toyota Avensis, bearing private hire plates, had pulled up in front of the hotel entrance. The driver was about to get out when Joe moved.

"You for Murray?" The driver nodded and Joe climbed in the back. "The police station, please."

"Right, boss." The driver set his meter going, slotted the car into gear, and turned it round, accelerating out of the car park. "You here for the weekend, are you?"

"Going home tomorrow," Joe replied.

"So what you down the nick for? Parking fine is it?"

"Something like that," Joe replied, and tried to apply his mind to the problem of Pitman's killing.

The driver was obviously disposed to conversation. "Bastards they are, mate. They nicked me this time last year on double yellows outside a paper shop in Ambleside. I told 'em me satnav was on the blink, but it still cost me seventy nicker. I meanersay, I'm a bleeding taxi driver, ain't I? Didn't make no difference though, did it? Still got a ticket. I told the warden, I said, 'What's up with you? Anniversary of the last time you saw your missus, or what?' Didn't make no difference. He still booked me."

Joe was no longer listening. His mind had ticked over onto a fresh track. Anniversary! Of course! That was what was wrong with Brenda. It was the anniversary of Colin's death.

Although he had known Brenda for many years, he had not known Colin half so well. He was older than Joe. He had attended their wedding and Colin's funeral, but it was before Brenda came to work at the Lazy Luncheonette so the in between bit was hazy. Brenda rarely spoke about him other than to insist that he would have approved of her freewheeling lifestyle. Sheila had told him that Colin wasted away over a period of months and even though his death was expected, it had still knocked the stuffing out of Brenda.

The curious thing was, Joe thought as the taxi swung along the main road towards Windermere, he had an idea Colin had passed away in the autumn, not the summer.

"Just shows you what a fickle friend memory is," he muttered.

"Wassat, mate?" the driver asked.

"Nothing," Joe replied. "Talking to myself."

"Know the feeling well."

Joe lapsed into silence again, rehearsing ways and means of bringing it up with Brenda when he got back to the Lakeside Manor.

Satisfied that he had learned at least part of the answer, he glanced out at the lake. Pushing seven thirty in the evening, the sun still blazed from just above the hills on the other shore, and the area was alive with people, thronging the shoreline. Living somewhere like this was always an attractive proposition when compared to life in an industrial area like Sanford, but Joe was smart enough to speculate on what it would be like in the murky depths of January, when snow would cover those same hills and the sun would disappear behind them as early as three in the afternoon.

Half a mile along the road, the driver pulled off to the right in front of an old, stone-built house, with a low level annexe added on to the right. There was sign to identify it as a police station, but the presence of two patrol cars in marked bays, and Inspector Perry's saloon, was enough. Joe paid the driver, walked up a short flight of stone steps to the door, which he found locked. Pressing the buzzer, he announced himself and with a click, it gave way.

Once inside, he found himself in a small reception area, a uniformed constable sat the other side reading the *Daily Mirror*.

"Joe Murray. Inspector Perry is expecting me."

"Yes, sir. I've told her you're here. She'll be with you in a minute."

Joe backed off to a bench by the door, and had barely sat down when an inner door opened, and Detective Constable Lesney appeared through the inner door.

"Hello, Mr Murray. Would you like to come through?"

She held the door open for him while he passed through into a bland corridor, its bare brick walls covered in dirty whitewash. A few doors along, she led him into a briefing room where Perry sat at a table, surrounded by full evidence bags, while she wrote a report. Facing the table, a large screen monitor had been hooked into a computer, and alongside it stood a video camera, its power light glowing red. The screen showed a similar but smarter, cleaner, recently decorated room, which Joe assumed was in Malé.

While Joe took a seat alongside Perry, Lesney busied herself at the kettle.

The inspector looked up from her paperwork and beamed a smile at him. "Ah, Joe. Welcome. We're in limbo at the moment. The flight has landed and the Malé police are waiting for Mr and Mrs Staines to come through immigration. They estimate about ten or fifteen minutes."

"No problem. Any news?"

"Nothing of any significance. You?"

He shrugged. "A few thoughts. That's all."

Perry put down her pen. "I'm listening."

"The overalls," Joe declared. "Did you happen to find a large bin bag anywhere near the body?"

"No."

"Then that probably lets out Rott and Wes. Harriet Atkinson, the dragon on the desk at the Lakeside Manor, insists that no one left the building wearing overalls. If it was Rott or Wes, they could have been carrying them, but again, Atkinson says not. And then, you have the problem of where did he change?"

"He was already wearing them," Perry replied, and when

128

Joe raised his eyebrows, she explained, "We've taken CCTV images from the boat station, and a man was seen in the distance wearing these overalls," she patted an evidence bag nearby, "or a pair very similar, at about the right time."

"Then I repeat, it can't have been either Rott or Wes."

"We think Mr Drummond is cleared," Lesney said. "We're still waiting for the full analysis, but it appears there was some kind of drug in his system. The best Scientific Support would say at the moment is that it was some kind of sleeper. We'll know for sure by morning."

"Which leaves us with Wes Staines," Perry said. "And I hear what you're saying, Joe, but there are ways and means round the problem. Wes could have stashed the overalls somewhere before he left the Lakeside Manor."

"Too complicated," Joe argued. "Yes, yes, all right, so you have to talk to him, but I think you're barking up the wrong tree."

"And you have another tree for us to bark up, do you?" There was no mistaking the challenge in Lesney's voice.

"Only speculation, and it involves drugs. But even if I'm right, it still only tells us why, not who." Joe eyed the collection of evidence and case notes on the table, paying particular attention to a collection of large photographs. He reached for them. "May I?"

Perry reached out and caught his hand. When he looked into her eyes, there was no severity, only concern.

"They're not very pretty, Joe."

He shook his hand free and picked up the pictures. "I've seen it all before."

The inspector was right. Those showing Pitman hanging and those of his body laid out, were brutal. Joe skimmed past them quickly, to study those of the boat shed.

He had been unable to visit the place physically while the police had it cordoned off as a crime scene, but the photographs, plus his recollections from the boat station, painted a sufficient picture.

The lakeshore was overgrown with reeds and grasses and the path from the boat station was well hidden, but the photographs picked it out clearly: a dirt track cutting its way through the untamed vegetation. Anyone approaching would be easily visible from the shed.

The place itself was built of timber, rotting in places, and obviously suffering from advanced neglect.

"How long since it was last in use?" Joe asked.

"About ten or fifteen years. Maybe less," Perry told him. "It's one of those places the council should have demolished, but they never seem to have the money or the will."

With a nod of understanding, Joe moved on to the next image – a wide angle view of the shed interior after Pitman's body had been removed.

The concrete floor was covered with the kind of detritus common to abandoned buildings; a few broken timbers, old newspapers, the remains of lakeside vegetation and what looked like bed sheets, and an old mattress. There were also plastic bags of various sizes and colours, including black bin bags.

"You said you hadn't found any," Joe objected after pointing them out.

"I assumed you meant new," Perry said. "Those had all been there a good while."

Again he nodded. "Lovers retreat is it?"

The inspector laughed. "Not at this time of year. During the darker months, probably, but right now it's light until almost ten in the evening and any couple, er, at it in there would be seen from the lake."

Joe smiled and moved on to the next picture.

It showed a member of Perry's forensic team, clad in a white jump suit, holding what looked like a surveyor's pole, to the right of which was a large hook fastened to a ceiling beam.

"His body was hanged from this hook?" Joe asked.

"Six feet eight inches from the floor," Perry agreed.

"Lets out Darlene, then," Joe said. "I mean, what is she? Five feet in carpet slippers? No way could she have lifted Pitman up that high. The same goes for Kelly."

"I think we said, Joe, if a woman is involved, she wasn't alone."

Joe studied the images again. There was something about the long shot of the shed which called to him. Almost as if he had seen it before.

It was entirely possible. He had visited this part of the world in the past, and he could well have seen the place, perhaps when it was still serviceable.

"Ma'am." Lesney gestured to the TV screen where Wes and Kelly, flanked by Maldives police officers, took their seats.

Joe brought his attention to bear as Perry collected up the photographs and said, "Let's deal with this and we can talk possibilities afterwards."

# Chapter Twelve

Both appeared tired. Wes had bags under his eyes, while Kelly had made some effort to brighten herself up with a fresh application of makeup, but her eyes still appeared red.

"I won't keep you long, Mr Staines, Mrs Staines," Perry announced. "Can you hear me all right?"

Both nodded.

"Can you hear us?" Wes asked, his voice coming from the speakers a split second after his lips moved, like a film out of sync.

"We hear you. I have Mr Murray with me, Mr Staines, and I believe he may have some questions for you, too."

Joe greeted them with a wave. "Hi Wes, Kelly."

"Hello, Mr Murray."

"Good flight?" Joe deliberately kept his approach conversational.

"Boring. Y'know," Wes replied. "A couple of hours to Spain is fine, but eleven rotten hours inside a tin can. It's too much. And it's not as if you can get any kip, either."

"Well, as I say, I won't keep you too long," Perry assured him. "Mr Staines, do you own an eighteen inch Stillson pipe wrench?"

"I have a few Stillsons," Wes replied. "Twelve, eighteen, twenty-four and thirty-six. Why?"

"Let's concentrate on the eighteen inch," Perry said. "Do you know where that wrench is?"

At the other end of the conversation, Wes shrugged. "In my van, I should think. It's not the kind of tackle you need on most jobs. It's only when you're working with large diameter pipes. Usually steel pipe, not copper. It's too heavy for copper, and too cumbersome for brass unions."

"Do you know when you last used it?" Perry demanded.

"Without checking the diary, I couldn't tell you." Wes's features became concerned. "It's a while back, for sure. Look, what is this? Have you got my Stillsons?"

"I don't know," Perry admitted. "How would you identify them as yours?"

"I always scratch my initial onto the lower part of the handle," Wes told her. "Usually just a 'W' but now and again I put 'WS' on them."

Perry passed the evidence bag containing the wrench to Lesney. She put on forensic gloves, removed the wrench from the bag, and then crossed to the video camera. With one eye on the monitor showing the camera feed, she juggled the position of the handle until the 'W' clearly showed.

"Can you see that, Mr Staines?"

"Yes I can."

"From that view, could you identify this wrench as your property?"

There was a moment's silence. "Hard to say. It looks like mine and that's how I mark my tools, but I'd need to see it, hold it before I could be sure. Listen, Inspector, are you saying —"

"We believe this piece of equipment was used to kill Adam Pitman," Perry interrupted as Lesney returned to her seat.

"Then someone must have nicked it from my van," Wes declared.

"Can you explain how that might happen, Wes?" Joe asked.

At the other end of the feed, Wes was still puzzled. "I don't know. It's not easy. We keep the van locked up at all times, even when we're on a job."

"Alarmed?" Perry asked.

"Well, yeah, but not when we're working. If we need tools

133

on a job, it'd be a proper pain having to kill the alarm every time we needed anything, so we just keep it locked without the alarm set."

"And have you left it anywhere like that recently? On a site or anything?"

"We don't do much work on sites, and yes it has been left like that when we work in peoples' homes, but we can keep our eyes on it."

Perry kept up the pressure. "So you're at a loss to explain how it could have been taken."

In Malé, Wes began to lose his cool. "If you're insinuating that Rott took it, then—"

"Our investigations have all but ruled out your partner, Mr Staines," Perry interrupted. "Which leaves us with person or persons unknown, but someone who could get hold of this wrench."

Wes exploded. He half stood and had to be restrained by one of the police officers with him. "Me? Listen, you stupid cow, I had nothing to do with it. I was at the bloody wedding reception all afternoon or in our room."

There was a brief hiatus while one of the officers in attendance warned him on his conduct. When they had done arguing, Wes faced the camera again.

"You're doing wonders here, Perry. I'm half a world away and threatened with arrest for verbally abusing you. It doesn't seem to matter what you're doing to me, though."

"I'm doing my job, Mr Staines. Asking questions to which I need answers. At this point, no one is accusing you, but our investigation is ongoing, and I may need to speak to you when you get back. For now, you remain a suspect."

Kelly sat forward. "Inspector, how are we supposed to enjoy our honeymoon with this hanging over us?"

"I would suggest, Mrs Staines, that you keep your mobile phone switched on at all times. That way, if I have any news, I can let you know." Joe tapped Perry on the arm, and she nodded. "I think Mr Murray wants a word," she said to the couple.

"Hiya, Kelly." Joe smiled encouragingly. "Before we go any further, I'll tell you I know neither you nor Wes had anything to do with this." He cast a quick sideways glance at Perry to see if there was any reaction, but apart from the vaguest tightening of her pursed lips, there was none. "By this time tomorrow, we should be able to clear the mess up and you can get on with enjoying yourselves. But to give us a chance, you have to tell me all you know about Adam Pitman."

"I've already told you, Mr Murray," Kelly replied. "I posed for him, he paid me peanuts and made a bit of money on the images. That's all. Darlene's the one to speak to. She had a thing with him for a while. But even she was glad to see the back of him eventually."

"When she came to Windermere, was she mad at Pitman?" Joe asked.

"Well, she was irritated by the way he kept pestering her. The texts. You know."

"Annoyed enough to kill him?"

Kelly appeared shocked. "She's not like that, Mr Murray."

"What about her brothers?"

"I don't know Jezz and Ricky that well, but they're a couple of dorks, really. They might be handy in a scrap, but I can't see them having the gumption to murder anyone." The set of Kelly's face told Joe she was becoming irritated now. "I think you're all barking up the wrong tree. Wes had no need to kill him. He didn't find out about me until after Pitman was killed. You should be looking elsewhere."

"Drug dealers for example?" Joe asked.

"That would be a start," Kelly insisted. "He was a known dealer round the campus. And then there was that other business, when he got arrested for murder."

Perry sat bolt upright, Lesney dropped her pen and Joe's eyes opened wide.

"Murder?" he demanded.

"Some girl was murdered in East London and he was charged with it, but it turned out he was innocent. I don't know all the details, but the girl's family were sure it was Pitman, and there was a hell of a row about it when he was acquitted."

"How long ago was this, Mrs Staines?" Perry demanded.

"I don't know. Five, six years back. It was all over the papers round Dagenham and Barking."

Alongside Joe, Lesney began to take hurried notes.

"And this was while you were at university?" he asked.

Kelly shook her head. "Just before I went there. I did my degree at Leicester, and I went to East London for my PGCE."

"Would Darlene know about it?"

Kelly shrugged. "I dunno. Maybe, maybe not. She's local to that area, but if she did, she never mentioned it when we were in uni, and she had no trouble dating Pitman."

Joe checked with the two policewomen, both of whom shrugged.

"You don't know any more than that, Mrs Staines?" Perry asked.

"You're the police. You should know about it."

Before another argument could follow, Joe cut in. "All right, Kelly. Listen, luv, you and Wes get off and enjoy your holiday. And don't worry. We'll get this mess cleared up."

On a signal from Perry, Lesney cut the connection.

"So, you didn't know about this murder business?" Joe demanded.

In the light of his disdain, Perry went on the defensive. "We would have got to it eventually. I told you this morning, we'd begun the process of checking on Pitman, and our work is still at a very early stage. Now that Kelly has put us onto it, I'll look it up, and we'll speak to the Met first thing in the morning." She chewed her lip. "Although how much we're likely to learn on a Sunday is anyone's guess."

"In that case, I'll get back to the Lakeside Manor and check it out on the internet."

"The police don't put details like that on the web, Mr Murray," Lesney pointed out.

Joe grinned. "No, but the papers do."

***

In contrast to the previous evening when the marquee had resounded to the thump of music and the floor had pounded under dancing feet, the hotel was an oasis of quiet when Joe got back. Most of the wedding guests had gone home, a few new arrivals were enjoying a drink on the lawns, and in the bar, Sheila, Brenda, and Lee and his family, were seated by the lawns' exit with Alec and Julia Staines, while behind the bar, Storm and the other bar staff idled away the time, polishing glasses.

Joe ordered a round of drinks to be delivered to the table and Storm began to set them up.

"Listen, lad, I need to speak to you about Adam Pitman."

"Is he the one who was, murdered?" Storm asked preparing a Campari and soda for Brenda.

Joe nodded. "Know him, did you?"

Storm shook his head. "I saw him at the Waterside on Thursday evening, of course. He was talking with Carl Vetch."

"Yeah, so I'm told. How about Darlene? Did you know her?"

Storm laughed. "I think everyone in Windermere knows Darlene, Mr Murray." He turned his back to pull a shot of gin from one of the optics. Rejoining Joe, he went on, "She has that kind of reputation."

"But you never dated her?"

The barman shook his head and put a half pint glass under the beer pump. "No, sir. We're, er, incompatible."

"Yeah, you're a Libra and she's a Virgo."

137

"Ah. Someone's told you."

"Rott," Joe agreed. "Is that the real reason?"

With the glass of beer filled, Storm put it on the bar. "I think Darlene was being, er, diplomatic when she told Mr Drummond that, sir. Truth is, I don't date women... if you take my meaning."

"I think so. You're from London, too. Did you know Darlene from down there?"

Storm shook his head, and added a pint of bitter to the tray. "No, sir, but it is a big city." He placed a brandy and ginger ale on the tray. "Is this going on your room, Mr Murray?"

"If you don't mind. One last thing. You still haven't told me why your parents christened you Storm?"

The young man laughed again. "You know my birth sign. I'll leave you to work it out. Would you like me to carry the tray to your table?"

"I'll manage, son."

Joe picked up the tray and joined his companions. Eager to hear his news, they listened while he gave them a rundown of events at the police station.

"So what are you saying, Joe?" Julia demanded "Wes is in the clear?"

"If you listened to me, Julia, you'd know I've been saying all along that Wes is innocent. No way did he kill this man. I don't think the police believe he did, either. All I'm saying – and the cops for that matter – is that Kelly's information has opened up another strand for investigation. They may still need to question Wes when he gets back from the Maldives, and he does have some explaining to do. It was his pipe wrench that was used to kill Pitman, and he needs to think about how it got from his van, where he insists it's locked up and secure, into the hands of the killer. On the other hand, the police also need to look into this business Kelly brought up, and I could do with talking to Darlene about it. It's a

138

possibility. Nothing more."

Julia clucked impatiently. "How is he supposed to enjoy himself with all this hanging over him?"

Joe suppressed his own irritation. "Oddly enough, I don't think most people are worried about that, Julia. I think they're more concerned with clearing his name. I will tell you this, though. If he and Kelly can come through this, they have a marriage that will last forever."

"Optimistic, Joe," Alec said.

"No. Common sense. Can you think of a worse start to married life? You find out your wife was a nude model for a sleazy photographer, then one of your tools was used to kill that photographer and you're suspected of it? I'm telling you, Alec, if they get through this, you have no need to worry about their future."

Rott entered the room and made for the bar. Joe called out to him, and he came over to them once he had collected a drink.

"Darlene not with you?" Joe asked.

"Just on me way to meet her at the boat station, Mr Murray. Her and her brothers were going for a meal at the Waterside." He waved at the five-star opulence around them. "Too expensive, this place."

"So they're not going home tonight?" Joe asked.

"Wes paid for us for tonight," Rott replied, "So we're all staying here until tomorrow lunchtime."

"I'll catch her in the morning then," Joe said. "Listen, she's never mentioned anything to you about some murder Pitman was charged with, has she?"

Rott nodded. "She's mentioned it. Few years back from all she says, and she reckons he was innocent anyway. London cops got it wrong. Summat like that."

"But it didn't frighten her off Pitman?"

"She says he was up front about it. There was nowt to be scared of." He took a hefty swallow of lager and checked his watch. "Better get going or she'll be nagging me on the phone. Catch you all later." He downed the rest of his drink, put the glass on a nearby table and left.

The group around the table murmured their responses and Rott disappeared.

"So where does that leave you, Joe?" Sheila asked.

"Up a gum tree. I have some research to do. I'll just grab a smoke, first." He stood up, and turned a benign eye on Brenda. "Listen, Brenda, I'm sorry. I've been a bit thick. I didn't realise it was the anniversary of Colin's death. Please forgive me."

Her face turned crimson with rage. "Colin," she hissed, "died in October." She stood up and flounced out of the room, leaving an astonished Joe staring after her.

"Is it me?" he asked.

All eyes were upon him, and he noticed that Sheila's and Alec's were good-humoured.

"I'm going for a smoke before I cause any more trouble."

Picking up his drink, he marched through the French windows and out onto the lawns. Finding a table nearby, he took out his tobacco and began to roll a cigarette.

Beyond the lake, the sky had turned pearly blue to white as the sun set. He could still see the gaily coloured lights of the boat station, picking out the crowds, and on the lake itself, boats moved this way and that, their dark silhouettes decked with lights, while various channels and buoys were marked out in red or green streamers, their reflections shimmering on the water.

For Joe, they highlighted the dark of his own fumbling. He could use some light to guide him to Pitman's killer and the source of Brenda's anger.

"You don't half know how to say the wrong thing, Joe."

Alec's voice, coming from the doorway, brought Joe back to reality.

Joe jammed the cigarette in his mouth and fished out his

lighter. "I'm an expert on the foot in the mouth technique, Alec." He lit up and went through the hacking routine, then sucked in a breath of the fresh, evening air. "You on your way home first thing?"

Alec sat down. Joe watched enviously as he, too, lit a cigarette, drew in a lungful of smoke and let it out with a hiss, but without a cough.

"We've been invited to Sunday lunch by Kelly's parents. They live up in Ambleside, so we're due there at half past one." Alec yawned. "After that, it's a three hour drive home, and the joys of working for a living first thing Monday morning."

"Tell me about it," Joe grunted. "Big job?"

"I have to quote for Sanford High School, and then I've a whole house redecoration on Leeds Road." Alec took another drag. "What about you? Straight home and early to bed tomorrow night?"

"Ha." Joe laughed cynically. "Chance'd be a fine thing. I've booked lunch here tomorrow, and like you we set off back. I reckon we'll make Sanford by, what… four o'clock. Then I've last week's books to balance, orders to sort out and I'll be up at five Monday morning to open up." He took a pull on the cigarette and helped ease the pressure on his lungs by taking a swallow of beer. "Between me, you and the gatepost, do you know what the hell is wrong with Brenda?"

"I'm not like you, Joe. I'm a one woman man."

"What the hell is that supposed to mean?"

Alec chuckled "I've made a point of keeping Brenda Jump at a virtual arm's length ever since Colin died. So, no, I don't know what's wrong with her. I do know that even mentioning Colin was dropping a prize brick, and getting the date wrong only made matters worse. But you were lucky. Brenda only tore you off a strip. If I did anything like that to Julia, she'd flay me alive, cut me into little pieces and feed them to the dog." His cigarette glowed in the gathering dark as he took another pull. "I thought you said you and Brenda were done… as an item, I mean."

"We are. It was never anything serious anyway, and it didn't so much come to a dead end as peter out. And I thought she was all right with that." He fumed a moment. "Bloody women. I'll never understand 'em if I live to be sixty." He took a deep drag on the cigarette and suffered another racking cough.

"By the sound of that hack, you'll be lucky to see fifty-seven, never mind sixty."

A shadow fell over the light coming from the bar. Alec crushed out his smoke, and glanced over his shoulder to see Brenda standing in the doorway. "Time for me to beat a tactical retreat, I think. Why not take a leaf out of your own book, Joe. You're always saying people are voice operated, so why not ask the woman herself what's wrong? See you in a bit."

Alec returned to the bar, passing Brenda with a muttered greeting. She walked across the lawn and sat alongside Joe.

"Brenda—"

"Don't say anything, Joe. Just listen instead."

Joe noticed the calm in her voice. There was none of the anger he had seen over the last few days. Its place had been taken by what sounded like sadness. He stubbed his cigarette in the ashtray and promptly took out his tobacco to roll another. "I'm listening."

"Do you know what it's like to watch someone waste away?"

Puzzled by her insistence that he listen, followed by a direct question, Joe was about to answer, but Brenda talked on.

"I do. I watched my husband wither from the man I married to a near skeleton, before he died. Towards the end, he was drugged up on morphine and he didn't know anything or anyone. He was an empty shell, wasting away. Even then, his death was a shock."

Joe risked a glance at her. He could see tears sparkling in

her eyes. Brenda, he reasoned, had always been the more emotional of his two companions.

She drew in a deep breath. "It's not something I would wish on anyone. I wouldn't wish the disease on my worst enemy, and neither would I like to see anyone suffer the agonies I did. It was a terrible, terrible time, and after he died, when I got over the shock, I was, I don't know… relieved, I suppose. Colin was beyond the pain, and I wouldn't have to sit there day after day, holding his hand, fighting my own pain down so I could talk to him."

She turned her head quickly and stared at Joe.

"It's not something I would want to go through again."

Joe shrugged and put the completed cigarette in his mouth. "I can understand that."

Her hard gaze remained fixed on him. "Then why am I going through it again?"

Lighter in hand, Joe paused. His brow furrowed. "Are you going through it again?"

"Yes. With you, you bloody idiot."

"Me?" Joe was so astonished he dropped his lighter on the table, from where it bounced to the grass. He bent to retrieve it, and as he sat up again, he had to pause for a moment to get his breath. "Brenda, I know we had a bit of a fling forty years ago, and we've had another over the last few months, but I'd hardly call it love. So why are you worrying about me?"

"It's not about love. It's not about sex. It's about friendship. We've known each other over fifty years. You think you mean nothing to me? You think I see you as another bed I can sleep in when I'm feeling my oats? It's more than that, Joe. You are my friend, and I'm watching you killing yourself with those little sticks of poison."

In the act of lighting his cigarette, Joe took a drag and coughed violently. "It's a smoker's hack. That's all."

"Yes, and when Colin's stomach started acting up, he said it was ulcers. When he began passing blood, he said it was haemorrhoids. I nagged him into going to the doctor but I nagged him too late. If I'd pushed him a year earlier, they might have caught it. He might still be with me. But you... You're doing nothing. I say nothing. In truth, you're smoking even more of those bloody coffin nails."

Her vehemence died with the same speed it had built up.

"Joe... Joe, please. Go to the doctor. Get it checked. Stop smoking. I don't want to watch you waste away the same as I watched Colin." Brenda leaned close to him and kissed him on the cheek. "You're a bad tempered shortarse, who can't even reach the top pie racks anymore, but you're our bad tempered shortarse and neither me nor Sheila want to lose you."

He stared out across the distant lake, his mind whirling with the things she had just said. Then he narrowed his focus on the cigarette. He crushed it out.

"The minute we get back to Sanford," he promised.

# Chapter Thirteen

With the time just after 5.00am, the tops of the hills opposite Joe's window glowed crimson in the early morning light. Bathed in shadow, the still waters of Lake Windermere were disturbed only by the ripples of birds floating and feeding.

Joe had spent most of his life getting out of bed at this hour, and the habit had become ingrained in his system to the point where he rarely needed an alarm clock. Even on a weekend outing, his body woke him as if ready for the Lazy Luncheonette fray.

The room remained largely in darkness. The sun was on the other side of the building and it would be some time before the strengthening daylight could dispel the night. Brenda lay sleeping in his bed. The soft rise and fall of her breasts reminding Joe of the passion they had indulged a few hours earlier.

The shock her admission had sent through him was genuine, as was his promise that he would do something about his smoking when they got back to Sanford. With the passage of several hours, reality intruded. He had never consciously tried to stop smoking, and he had the feeling that he would not do so this time, either. He was grateful for Brenda's concern and for the end to her irritation, but he knew himself well enough to know that he would carry on as always.

And in the meantime, he had a murder to deal with, and friends to clear of suspicion.

Soft light from his netbook screen penetrated the shadows in the room, and on the screen was a post from a newspaper dated eight years previously, its headline screaming, *ELLEN CARTWRIGHT MURDER, LOCAL MAN ARRESTED!*

He had run a simple, Google search on *Adam Pitman murder charge*, which had turned up the usual plethora of meaningless results, but amongst them Joe spotted the piece from an East London newspaper, the *Dagenham & Romford Gazette*. Employing sensationalist tabloid language, it revelled in the kind of ghoulish interest murders always attracted.

*Local glamour photographer, Adam Pitman (30) has been taken to Dagenham Police Station for questioning on the murder of Ellen Cartwright.*

*It's one week since vivacious Ellen's body was found in her flat off Ripple Road, and acting on information received from the public, police moved swiftly last night to take Pitman into custody. Speaking outside the police station, Detective Chief Inspector Robert Keenan, leading the investigation, told reporters, "It's too early to say whether or not Mr Pitman was involved in this brutal killing, but we need to question him on the matter."*

*The savage manner of Ellen's death sent shockwaves through the community. A fun-loving and attractive woman aged 23, she was popular with friends and neighbour alike…*

Joe cut the page off there. He had no desire to continue reading through the usual, trite opinions of neighbours who, even if the girl had been the vampire from Hell, would have spoken of her shining like an angel.

He ran the Google search again, this time altering it to *Adam Pitman charged*. The same result popped up, along with other items from national newspapers. Amongst them he picked up a single report, again from the *Dagenham & Romford Gazette*, and clicked on the link.

*PITMAN CHARGED.*

*Photographer Adam Pitman was, last night, charged with the brutal murder of Ellen Cartwright.*

*Ellen, of Ripple Road, was found beaten to death in her flat almost two weeks ago, and since then an all-out effort from the police resulted in the arrest of the glamour photographer. He will appear before Dagenham magistrates tomorrow morning, and is expected to be remanded for trial.*

Again Joe returned to Google and ran a further search, this time searching for *Pitman trial*. Although it returned many entries, a single one leapt at him from the screen.

*PITMAN ACQUITTED*, read the headline.

*The date was almost a year after the previous piece, and again, the newspaper went into great detail.*

*Adam Pitman was acquitted of the murder of Ellen Cartwright. In a sensational turnaround, it emerged that Detective Sergeant Michael Hancock, one of the investigating officers tampered with evidence in order to improve the chances of a conviction. The judge called both counsel to his chambers and when they returned to the court, the jury was ordered to find Pitman not guilty.*

*In a statement outside the court, defence counsel, Desmond Jones, QC, said, "My client has insisted upon his innocence all along, and it is now clear that what the police described as an open and shut case, was in fact built upon manufactured evidence."*

*Pitman had nothing to say other than he wished to be left in peace to return to his life and work, and make an effort to pick up his career.*

*It's over a year since the body of 23-year-old Ellen was found bludgeoned to death in her apartment off Ripple Road…*

Joe stopped reading and went back to his search, but this time, he entered *Ellen Cartwright murder* in the box, and hit the enter key.

There were many more results this time, including items from the BBC and other TV news channels, but it was a further entry from the *Dagenham & Romford Gazette* which caught Joe's eye.

*FATHER OF MURDERED WOMAN COMMITS SUICIDE.*

*It was dated only three weeks after Pitman's acquittal.*

*Norman Cartwright, the 56-year-old father of murdered Dagenham woman, Ellen Cartwright, has taken his own life.*

*A police spokesperson said they were called to the family home in Barkingside early this morning, where they found Mr Cartwright's body hanging from an overhead beam in the garage. They are not looking for anyone else in connection with the incident. His wife and 16-year-old son were being comforted by friends and neighbours.*

*Mr Cartwright had expressed his disgust at the acquittal of Adam Pitman, a local photographer who stood trial for Ellen's murder, but who was found not guilty after it was discovered that one of the investigating officers had tampered with evidence.*

*"Right up to his death, Norman was convinced that Adam Pitman murdered Ellen and got away with it," a neighbour told us.*

*Mr Pitman was unavailable for comment, but his solicitor said, "Mr Cartwright's death is regrettable, and my client's sympathies go to the Cartwright family."*

Joe shut down the internet, and sat back, staring through the window, out into the dawn, piecing together the things he had just learned and slotting them into the complex jigsaw of Pitman's murder. Stepping out onto the balcony, he rolled a cigarette, lit it, and in deference to Brenda still sleeping, suppressed the usual coughing fit as much as he could before sitting back, and once more gazing into the growing daylight, the gears of his active mind slowly meshing to formulate the theory.

There were many gaps, but with the time coming up to half past five he took out his mobile, hesitated a moment, and then rang Perry's number.

"Inspector? It's Joe. Joe Murray."

She sounded distant and sleepy. "Joe? What... have you seen the time."

"I know it's early but I've been doing some research on that story Kelly told us about Pitman," he replied. "Have you looked into it yet?"

"I pulled the case from the database last night."

"Then you know all about the Ellen Cartwright murder and how Pitman got off."

"Yes. We know, but there's nothing to suggest that it's relevant. It all happened in London, and I don't know that any of the Cartwright family have moved up here. Or do you know differently."

"No, I don't, but I wouldn't, would I? I don't live in these parts. I will tell you what struck me when I read up on it all, though. Ellen Cartwright was clubbed to death, and her father hanged himself. Adam Pitman was clubbed to death and then hanged." He paused to let the information permeate. "Still think there's no link?"

There was a long and telling silence; so long that Joe began to think the connection had died, but as he was about to check, Perry spoke.

"I see what you're saying. It's also possible that someone is making it appear that way. I'll get onto it when I get to the station in about four hours. What time are you leaving tomorrow... correction; today?"

"After lunch. We have to open up on Monday morning."

"In that case, I'll see you at the Lakeside Manor between eleven and twelve in the morning. Goodnight, Joe."

The connection died. The word 'goodnight', said with the dawn gathering in intensity, caused Joe to smile ruefully at the phone for a moment, before he shut it down, and returned to the room to switch off the netbook.

He looked at Brenda's sleeping form and a satisfied smile crept across his face. Now there was a *real* woman. Never mind your nude models in provocative poses which practically shouted, 'Come on, big boy, do your worst'. Give him the lights out and an experience woman like Brenda...

His lusty thoughts ground to a halt.

Nude models. Provocative poses. Locations. Cerne Abbas, Angel of the North, a stone pub with a beer garden and an old shed/workshop.

He returned to the netbook, switched it back on and, stepping back out onto the balcony, rolled a cigarette. He puffed agitatedly at it while waiting for the computer to go through its slow start routines. With it barely half smoked, he crushed it out in the ashtray and hurried back in.

Going online, he went straight to Pitman's website, and the gallery. Scrolling quickly through the images, cursing himself for not having bookmarked them earlier, he found the images of Darlene, and began to open up the thumbnails, one by one. He was not interested in the fertility symbolism of the Cerne Abbas Giant, nor the huge, steel structure of the Angel of the North. Instead he homed in on a beer garden, a stone-built pub and a ramshackle old shed.

A broad grin spread across his face.

*GOTCHA!*

Almost six hours had passed since his conversation with Perry when Joe walked into the Waterside Inn, to find the place quiet, but ready for the fray.

He had not been entirely idle. After a breakfast with Sheila and Brenda, noticeable for its lighter, more convivial mood, his two companions had invited him on another shopping expedition to Windermere, but he had declined. Lee and Cheryl were taking Danny to the boat station for a last look around before their afternoon departure, but again, Joe had passed.

Instead, he had returned to his room, packed his belongings, then made use of the hotel's colour printer, to run off copies of some of the photographs from Pitman's website. Tom Nelson and Harriet Atkinson had kept a beady eye on him while he did so, and her face had disfigured into a mask of disgust when she saw the content of the images.

"It's for the cops," Joe told her. "Believe me, I find this stuff

150

as disagreeable as you, but in a case like this, it's needs must."

His words did little to mollify Mrs Atkinson, and he came away convinced that her opinion of him, already low, had sunk even further.

With the prints safely stored in a large envelope, Joe made his way through the bottom gate and along the road to the Waterside, and approached Bernard Vetch.

"Is your boy about?"

"You here again, are you, Mr Murray? You wanna be careful, or you'll end with a taste for our beer."

Joe was in no mood for distraction. "In about ten minutes, Vetch, I call Inspector Perry and tell her what I know. Stop fooling around and get your boy out here."

Carl Vetch's voice reached him from behind. "And what makes you think you'll be able to call the cops?"

Memories of the intimidation he had suffered in Weston-super-Mare earlier in the year assailed Joe. He quelled the tremor inside, turned and leaned casually against the bar. Looking the younger Vetch up and down, he said, "What makes *you* think you can stop me?"

Stocky, as muscular as his father was portly, Carl smacked one fist into the opposite palm. "I can stop you."

"The way you stopped Adam Pitman?" Joe smiled. He felt no humour. It was an empty gesture designed to lend an air of insouciant disregard. He held up his envelope. "Pictures proving you lied to me, sonny. Now, you may be bigger than me, and you may be able to stop me calling the cops, but do you think I'm as stupid as you? I got these from the internet, and the police will know before long where to find them and what they mean. It's all on my computer back at the Lakeside Manor. Cut the big bully boy act, and start talking."

"I dunno what you mean by the way I stopped Pitman, but you won't be around to see the police get hold of them pictures."

Carl took a pace forward and Joe's heart began to pound.

"I think he will."

Relief flooded Joe. The Vetches turned to face Maddy at the bar, sorting through her purse.

She spoke to the landlord. "I'd like to settle my bill, please, but before you do, you'd better warn your boy I have a black belt in karate and if he makes one silly move against my friend, Joe, I'll deck him." She smiled sweetly at the two men.

"Now," Joe said. "Do we talk, or do I pop in to see Perry?"

Vetch senior frowned and glanced around the bar at his staff getting the place ready. "Not here. Out in the garden. I'll be two minutes."

"Both of you," Joe warned and headed for the beer garden exit.

He chose the table he and Maddy had taken the day before, and looked towards the lake.

Opening his envelope, he took out one of the photographs and ignoring Darlene's display of her body, studied the background. The trees in the image were barren, their branches devoid of foliage, and the barrels supporting closed parasols appeared damp, as if they had suffered a rainstorm earlier in the day. From the blue sky in the background, Joe knew that it had not rained. The picture had been taken in winter, and those barrels had been frosted over earlier.

When he compared the image to the reality before him, the position of the barrels and the trees gave him an exact match.

"Pretty girl," Maddy said as she joined him. "I wish I had the nerve to get my kit off like that, but what I have under my clothing wobbles a lot more than hers."

Joe chuckled. "Promise me you'll let me find out sometime."

She wagged a finger at him. "I never make promises I don't intend to keep." She sat alongside him. "So, Joe, are you into soft porn as a matter of course, or is this just a one off?"

"I'm not remotely interested in it," Joe told her, "but young Vetch lied to me yesterday, and this picture proves it." He glanced back at the doorway where Vetch was barking orders back at his staff. "Do you really have a black belt?" he asked Maddy.

"Oh yes. It looks brilliant when I wear it with a spectacular red outfit I have at home."

She smiled and Joe laughed as he tucked the photograph back in the envelope.

Each carrying a beaker of coffee, Vetch and his son joined them, and from the outset, it was obvious that the older man was in no mood for dallying.

"Right, Murray, what the hell is this all about?"

"It's about you and your son here trying to fool everyone. You made it sound as if you didn't know Pitman. You also made it sound as if Pitman was just asking if you knew Darlene and you could maybe help find her."

"That's right," Carl said. "He just—"

"Cut it out," Joe interrupted. "You both knew Pitman. He'd been here before."

"I deny that," Vetch snapped.

Joe removed the three images, laid them on the table and turned them to face the father and son. "Then how do you explain these pictures taken in your beer garden and in front of your pub?"

His question was greeted with stunned silence.

"Don't try to fob me off with the 'I didn't know' routine, either. There is no way Darlene could have stripped off in your back yard without you knowing about it." Joe pointed to the third image, of the old boathouse. "And he'd also been to the boathouse before. So, too, had Darlene."

Carl looked worried, but his father was less concerned.

"All right, so we knew Pitman. He stayed here. What of it?"

"I'll tell you what of it," Joe retorted. "While he was here, he offered one of you the Delaney of a lifetime. Probably you." He pointed at Carl. "Give him fifty notes for these little bags of white powder, and he'd guarantee you'd double your money overnight, and you'd create instant demand. And no matter how much you wanted, he could supply."

The colour drained from Carl's face, and Joe knew he had it right.

"He came back again a couple of days ago carrying a large stash, but you couldn't cut the deal here. Not in a pub full of people, so you agreed to meet him at the old boathouse, but you had no intention of paying him. You'd already nicked the overalls and pipe wrench from Rott and Wes's vans when they worked here, and you knew the wedding was on, so you told him exactly where he could find Darlene, knowing it would throw everyone on the wrong track. You spiked Rott's drink and Darlene's to make them sleep, and in the gap between the reception and evening disco, you met him and killed him."

Carl looked as if he wanted to run, but still Vetch appeared in control of both himself and his son. Joe waited to hear their response.

"That big lad at the reception," Vetch said eventually. "You said he was your nephew."

Puzzled, Joe nodded. "That's right."

"I only spoke to him once or twice on Friday," Vetch admitted, "but is he as gormless as he sounds?"

"He can be," Joe admitted. "But then, when I was his age, I think I was pretty gormless, too."

"And me. Well, Carl is the same. A good lad at heart, but thick as a brick sometimes." Vetch sighed. "You're right, Murray. Pitman stayed here about three years back, and he had that little tart, Darlene with him. He asked permission to take his filthy pictures in the beer garden. Told us they were for a calendar and we'd get a mention. So I said yes. It was the middle of January, trade was slack, and as a businessman you know that any advertising is welcome, even if it is a little slut flashing her boobs in your beer garden."

The landlord sighed, and took a drink from his beaker.

"And you're right about the cocaine, too. Pitman offered

Carl the deal of the century, but it wasn't fifty quid's worth, it was a coupla hundred." He turned angry features on his son. "And this daft bugger fell for it."

"It was a business deal, Dad," Carl protested.

"It was criminal, you idiot," Vetch snapped. Taking a breath to calm down, he spoke to Joe again. "But that is as far as it went. I found that cocaine and flushed it down the lavatory. All of it." He glared at Carl. "And if he'd been younger, I'd have walloped him. As it is, I warned him never to do anything so bloody stupid again, and he never has. That, Murray, is as far as it all went."

Joe absorbed the information. "You abandoned your bar yesterday, leaving it to staff, while you supervised the reception."

"Yes. And I made sure Carl was with me, so I could keep an eye on him and Pitman. And you were also wrong about Wes and Rott's vans. Rott worked here, sure, but Wes never did, and when their vans were here. They were locked up. I don't know what all this business about pipe wrenches and overalls is, but it's nothing to do with me or Carl."

Again Joe fell silent, churning over the information.

He turned on Carl. "What did he say to you on Thursday night? The conversation Maddy saw?"

"He asked whether Darlene would be in. I told him I hadn't seen her for yonks. He asked me where she lived. I told him I didn't know, and he threatened me with the law, so I told him she'd be at the wedding on Friday."

"Makes sense, Joe," Maddy said. "I told you the conversation was serious."

Joe again rounded on Bernard Vetch. "Tell me this, then. You knew what Pitman was about, yet you let him stay here. Why?"

"He gave us no choice," Vetch admitted. "He knew that if she went anywhere for a drink, Darlene would come here. It was the only place he and she knew in this area. When he turned up he demanded a room and said if I didn't give him one, he'd bell the police and tell them Carl was a drug dealer."

Again, it made sense to Joe and he said so. "It also gives you another motive for killing him," he added.

"You're not listening, Murray," Vetch retorted. "We did not kill Pitman. I can't say I'm sorry to see the back of him, but it had nothing to do with us."

"So where were you between three and six on Friday afternoon?"

"Most of the time we were at the the Lakeside Manor," Vetch replied. "I came back here about five o'clock to make sure everything was running smoothly, and I was back there in time to open up at seven."

"Which still gives you plenty of time to kill him."

Vetch drank the rest of his coffee and stood up. "Do what you want, Murray. You seem to have made up your mind that I'm guilty, or Carl is, so do as you like. Call the cops. You can't prove one damn word and do you know why? Because neither of us is guilty. Now, if you'll excuse us, we have a bar to run."

He snapped his fingers and like a faithful dog, Carl followed his father back into the pub.

Joe gathered his photographs together and put them back in the envelope.

"He's right, you know, Joe," Maddy said.

"Hmm What?"

"Vetch. He's right. It all makes a sort of sense, but you can't prove a thing, and ten to one, he'll have plenty of witnesses to swear that he was here between five and seven on Friday night."

"I was so sure…" Joe stood up ready to leave. "You on your way, Maddy?"

With a nod, she, too, stood and accompanied him through the bar, where, under a steely glare from Vetch, they made their way out to the front car park.

She paused by her Vauxhall Corsa. "Cases in the boot,

research saved to laptop, gotta get home before the weather breaks. Been fun meeting you Joe, and don't forget, if you're ever in Scarborough—"

"I know. Give you a call."

# Chapter Fourteen

"Detective Sergeant Michael Hancock altered a single detail on Pitman's Statement, and it was enough to call into question the entire police evidence. After some deliberation and meeting with both counsel, the trial judge ordered the jury to find the defendant not guilty, and Pitman was acquitted."

Listening to Perry, Joe took in a lungful of smoke and let it out with a hiss. He paused a moment, waiting for the inevitable coughing fit, but it did not come.

They were at a table on the lawns, enjoying the hot weather. Joe, Sheila and Brenda had dressed casually, sensibly, ready for the three hour journey home, while Perry maintained the smart yet uncomfortable-looking formality of business wear.

After listening to Perry, Joe asked, "The detail being?" "It's complicated," Perry admitted. "Ellen Cartwright was murdered sometime between ten p.m. and one a.m. In his statement, Pitman claimed to have been in the Engine House pub, on Ripple Road, until eleven p.m. That still put him in the frame, and even though the rest of the evidence was not overwhelming, the police had no qualms about charging him. Sergeant Hancock then changed the eleven to a ten."

Joe gaped. "And no one noticed?"

"No one," the inspector agreed. "It was a tiny detail. Hancock later said, he was trying to ensure that Pitman was convicted by giving greater credibility to the time he had available to commit the crime. The defence counsel only picked it up during the trial when he was briefing Pitman for his turn on the stand. Pitman immediately denied having said that. The original statement was brought out, a graphologist looked it over and confirmed that the second 'one' in the time had been changed to a zero. The defence then called into question the whole of the police evidence and at length the judge agreed."

"What other evidence did they have against Pitman?" Brenda asked.

"Not much, but enough, or so the Crown Prosecution Service thought. There were traces of Pitman all over the flat, but he never denied that he and Ellen Cartwright had had a relationship. He was seen entering her flat that night at about midnight. He never denied that either, but he maintained that he had called, couldn't get an answer and left, and he was seen leaving about a quarter of an hour later."

"Were there any traces of him on the murder weapon?" Sheila asked.

"No," said Perry, "But that's because the murder weapon was never found. Forensics indicated a heavy implement, similar to the one used on Pitman. Obviously, there were no traces of Ellen's blood or skin on Pitman, but again there wouldn't be. A week had passed between her death and his arrest. He lied several times during his interviews. He claimed the reason he did not come forward when she was murdered was because he was out of the country, but it wasn't true. When Chief Inspector Keenan checked, he was seen in the Engine House several times during that week. Eventually he admitted he had not left the country, but he didn't come forward because he was frightened. He also claimed that his relationship with Ellen was over and that she had been pestering him. Mobile phone records indicated that it was the other way round. He had been pestering her. All in all, the police and the CPS thought they had a good case and it went to trial. It was going well, too. They were certain of a conviction until the altered evidence turned up."

"So what happened to this Sergeant Hancock?" Joe wanted

to know.

"He went through disciplinary procedures and he was fired eventually."

"He wasn't prosecuted?" Sheila asked.

"No. He could have been. Falsifying evidence is a serious offence, and he could have been jailed for it, but he had a good record prior to that, and the disciplinary hearing recommended dismissal only. He had acted with the best of intentions. Naturally, that doesn't make it any the less of an offence, and most of his colleagues, while they were annoyed with him, understood his motives."

Joe slotted the information into the relevant compartments of his brain. "And what's happened to him since he got fired?"

Perry frowned. "Hazy. He managed to get a job as a security man in a shopping precinct, but didn't hold it down long. He disappeared for a while, then came back to the area, but he was unemployed. Then, suddenly, about a year ago, he left again and hasn't been seen since."

Joe stroked his chin thoughtfully, and took another drag on his smoke. "A year ago. Just about the time Darlene Garbutt moved up here from the same area."

The three women concentrated on him.

"What are you suggesting, Joe?" Brenda demanded.

Relieved that she was no longer treating him with contempt, he said, "Let me paint you a picture. Just suppose Pitman is guilty of Ellen Cartwright's murder. But he has something on Hancock. It may be women, it may be drugs, it may be, I dunno, gambling, or whatever. The trial is coming up. Pitman gets to Hancock somehow. Maybe the sergeant has to see him while he's on remand. He presents Hancock with whatever hold he has over him. In order to keep Pitman's mouth shut, Hancock is asked to make a change to the statement. Nothing major. Just change the time Pitman says he left the pub. Don't make it obvious, but make sure it can be uncovered. That way Pitman gets off. Hancock gets fired, for

160

sure, but it's preferable to facing up to whatever Pitman has on him. Now fast forward a few years. Hancock is out of work and he's an angry man. He tails Pitman everywhere, gets to know as much as he can about him, his work, his girlfriends, everything. Then he starts playing with mobile phones. He sends messages to Darlene, supposedly from Pitman. He sends messages from Pitman, supposedly from Darlene. His aim is to kill Pitman and use Darlene or her brothers as the patsies for the murder. Darlene comes up here. Even better for Hancock. No one knows him in the Lake District. He follows her and the text messages start again, then, joy of joy, Darlene is to be a bridesmaid for Kelly. Posing as Darlene, he sends a final text to Pitman, warning him that unless he shows up here with a large wedge of money, she's gonna do a bit of muck spreading with what she knows about him."

Joe fell silent for a moment and Perry picked up the thread.

"Darlene thinks it's Pitman, and vice versa, when all along it's Hancock. That explains the argument you overheard, Joe. The one between Pitman and Darlene's brothers. Hancock then lures him to the boat house and brains him." She considered the idea. "It's possible. A bit long-winded, but it could explain a lot."

"But how could he know that Darlene and Paul would sleep through the afternoon on Friday?" Sheila asked.

Crushing out his cigarette, Joe gestured at Perry.

"Zolpidem, Mrs Riley," the inspector said. "The urine sample from Paul Drummond revealed traces of the drug. It's a sleeping pill. Quite potent, too, and when mixed with alcohol, it's almost guaranteed to knock the user out."

"Prescription drug?" Brenda asked, and when Perry nodded, she went on, "So how did Hancock get hold of it?"

"Too easily, if you want my opinion," Joe said. "Here's a bloke out of work, down on his uppers, and he goes to his GP, saying, 'I'm not sleeping, doc'. Like all the NHS crowd, the doctor is under pressure, so he writes out a prescription. 'Take one of those every night before you go to bed'. Simple."

Perry agreed. "I don't necessarily go along with Joe's opinions on the NHS, but it's not difficult."

Seeking to avert an argument before it could begin, Sheila said, "I'm sure Joe was referring to the pressure under which GPs work, and not criticising the NHS as an institution." Drawing a breath, she went on, "To do that, Hancock must have been at the wedding, even if he only sneaked in."

"Again, not difficult," Joe ventured. "It was a busy time, there were people dancing, chatting, moving around. Anyone dressed like they were guests at a wedding, could have wandered into the marquee, and dropped the pills in Rott's drink. Darlene's too, if you think about it. No one would have noticed." He turned to Perry. "Did you run a urine test on Darlene?"

The inspector shook her head. "Not yet. She's a busy girl and we haven't caught up with her yet. We left a message at reception, but she hasn't got back to us."

"Won't it be too late now?" Brenda asked.

Perry was hazy. "Maybe, maybe not. That stuff can stay in the body for anything up to forty-eight hours."

"There is another possibility," Joe said. "The Cartwright family? Or what was left of it. Ellen's mother and her brother."

Perry smiled. "How did you know she had a brother? The newspaper reports never mentioned him."

"One of them did, as a matter of fact," Joe replied. "It said he was sixteen at the time, so he'd be about twenty four now."

"Indeed he will," Perry replied. "Orkan Cartwright was, I think, sixteen at the time Ellen was killed. When you brought all this up on the phone last night, Joe, I had my people run a check on them. He and his mother continued to live in the family home. She lost her mind when her husband committed suicide, and the boy looked after her for a while. Then he just disappeared and she was found dead. Overdose. I saw the coroner's report."

162

"How long ago?" Joe asked.

"About a year."

"Again, just about the same time Hancock disappeared and Darlene moved north. What price Hancock killed the boy and the old woman?"

"Why would he?" Brenda asked. "They were no threat to him."

"Not so, Mrs Jump," Perry declared. "After Norman hanged himself, Mrs Cartwright, acting through her son and the family lawyer, campaigned to have Pitman retried, and for Hancock to face a court of law. If we accept Joe's analysis of the situation, had that trial come about, Hancock may well have gone to prison for a long time. Especially after what was found in his flat after he went missing."

Joe raised his eyebrows. "Drugs?"

Perry nodded. "Cocaine. A sizeable amount. Hundreds of thousands of pounds worth."

"That's probably what Pitman had on him," Joe speculated. Leaning forward, he opened his tobacco tin and began rolling another cigarette under the scathing glances of the three women. "This thing looks more likely by the minute. Just a few loose ends. First off, how did he get hold of the pipe wrench and Rott's overalls?"

"We don't know. Right now, it's just another strand of the investigation, and we've barely begun on it."

"Okay." Joe licked the gummed edge of the cigarette paper and completed the roll-up. Jamming it in his mouth, digging into his gilet for his Zippo, he asked, "Who was he?"

The question produced frowns from all three women. "Michael Hancock, Joe," Brenda reminded him. "You know. A disgraced bobby, who—"

"No, no. You don't understand. I mean who was he at the wedding? He could hardly walk in and say, I'm Michael Hancock and I'm here to incriminate your best man and chief bridesmaid. There were plenty of people taking videos at the wedding on Friday afternoon. Could the police records help us to identify him at the wedding?"

"They might," Perry said. "Obviously, we have photographs of him on file."

"Did he have to be posing as a guest?" Sheila asked. "Could he be a member of staff, or one of the outside caterers who dealt with the reception?"

"How old was he?" Joe asked Perry.

"Right now he would be about forty-five," the inspector replied.

"Nelson, then," Joe suggested. "The hotel manager."

Perry shook her head. "Tom Nelson has been here for the last twenty years to my knowledge. Probably longer."

"Well it rules out people like Storm and although I'd love it to be Harriet Atkinson, I have to say Hancock would have to be a master of disguise to pull that off."

"The simple fact is, Joe, we don't know who he might have been, or even if it is him. We'll be looking at CCTV images for the actual wedding day to see if we can spot him."

Joe drummed his fingers on the table. "Well, that just about sums up everything I know. Unless anyone else has any ideas, I'm stumped."

"I never thought I'd see the day," Sheila said with a broad smile.

"Odd name that."

All eyes turned to Brenda. "Again?" Joe invited.

"Orkan. I was just saying it was an odd name."

"Swedish, Danish," Sheila told her. "Northern European, anyway. Roughly translated as hurricane." She smiled again. "The boy was probably fast on his feet."

Joe's blood ran cold. "Oh, for God's sake, now I get it."

The voice of Lee reached him from the car park. He looked over his shoulder to where his nephew was shaking hands with Rott as the latter loaded the boot of his car. Darlene sat in the car reading a newspaper as Rott prepared to get in.

Joe got to his feet. "Look sharp or we'll miss them." He hurried off to the car park, followed by the three women.

"Rott," he called out. "It's been great seeing you again, son." Joe offered his hand and Rott shook it. "You on your way?"

"Another few minutes, Mr Murray."

Joe eyed Darlene. "Checking your stars are you, Darlene?"

She gave him a sickly smile. "I always do, Mr Murray."

Joe nodded. "I wish I had that kind of guidance." He turned to Rott. "Fancy staying for lunch? My treat. We're not leaving until about half past three."

Rott glanced at Darlene and raised his eyebrows.

She looked diffident. "I, er, I don't know. I'm not, er..."

"Great," Joe said. "Lee, I need to talk to Rott. Why don't you and Darlene go back into the hotel and tell them there'll be an extra two for lunch."

"All right, Uncle Joe. Come on, Darlene."

Suspicion haunting her eyes, Darlene climbed out of the car and followed Lee into the hotel.

"You're well in there, Rott," Joe commented watching Darlene's lithe body sway along behind Lee.

"Have to see, Mr Murray."

"Yeah. Course. You take your time, lad. Listen, Rott, I was just talking with the inspector, here, and we think we know what's been going on. We believe it's a former policeman, but what we can't figure out is how he got hold of your overalls and Wes's pipe wrench. We guess he must have nicked them from the back of your van."

Rott shook his head and slammed down the boot of his car. "Didn't Wes tell you, Mr Murray? We always keep it locked up."

"Always?"

"Always. Specially when we're working on a site. Proper thieving toe rags, those site workers."

"Hmm." Not for the first time Joe stroked his chin, his mind working over the facts. "We know they didn't take them here. Wes told us they were in the van, not either of your cars. That means they had to have been taken from the back of your van, and quite recently, or you'd have missed them. Tell me, have you had any, er, strange jobs come in over the last week or two?"

Rott laughed. "They're all strange in this part of the world. People with tons of money all wanting the job done for a pound... Oh, wait a minute. There was that gas leak on Wastwater Street last Monday. We got a call out late at night. Me and Wes went down there, and the old boy who owned the place said he didn't know what we were talking about. We had a right argument with him, but he threatened to call the cops, so we came away."

"You went in the van? Not your own cars?"

Rott nodded. "Wes picked me up. We had to. All the tools are in the van."

"And the van was never out of your sight?"

"Nope... well, it was parked out front and we were round the side of the house, but it was all locked up. No one could have got in. We'd have known."

"Oldest trick in the book," Perry said. "Get you where they want you, and normally they would be away with your van while you were distracted with the householder. This time, they wanted something in the van. Who knows what kind of tools you keep in there?"

Rott shrugged. "We only leave the heavy duty stuff in the van. I'm telling you, they couldn't have got in. They'd have needed a key. If they didn't, they'd have to force the doors and we'd have noticed."

"Who has keys to the van, Rott?" Joe asked.

"We each have our own vans and our own keys, but we also have spares for both vans. There's spare sets at Wes's house and another at mine. I keep 'em in a cupboard with my DVDs and stuff."

"And that spare set is still there?" Joe demanded.

"It was the last time I looked."

"Which was when?"

Rott shrugged. "I dunno. But I haven't been burgled or anything. Sorry, Mr Murray, but I think you've got it wrong."

A shock of realisation shot through Joe. A broad smile crossed his face. "No, son, you've got it wrong. You trusted someone and they let you down. And suddenly, I think I know who and how." He glanced at the hotel. "Inspector, call your people and tell them to get some bodies out here. Enough to make a few arrests." He strode away. "Come on. Let's all get a beer."

The inspector took out her phone, and with a frown of puzzlement as deep as anyone else's, followed him.

Joe led them into the bar where Lee, Cheryl and Danny were seated with Darlene and her brothers. At the bar, Storm busied himself stocking the chillers, while Nelson checked spirit bottles and optics.

"Storm," Joe said to the barman, "Drinks for the whole table, please, and add it to my bill. I have a long drive home, so I'll just have a glass of lemonade."

"Sure thing, Mr Murray."

There was a short delay while Storm took the orders from everyone, and Joe, Sheila, Brenda, Rott and the inspector settled in around the table.

Eventually, Joe held court.

"Quite a puzzling affair this one, but I've just worked it out. I know who did it and how. I also know who helped the killer." Joe laid a beady eye on the Garbutt brothers.

"Perhaps, then, you'd be good enough to explain it to me, Joe," Perry invited, putting her phone away. "Before my people arrive."

"No problem. First off, what you have to do is forget all about coincidences. It was no coincidence that Detective Sergeant Hancock disappeared at the same time as Darlene moved up here. It was no coincidence that Ellen Cartwright's

167

mother died at about the same time. It was all part of the plan that was probably designed to extract revenge on Adam Pitman for Ellen's murder. Or at least, that's how it started."

Perry was shocked. "Hancock killed Ingrid Cartwright, too?"

"No. He didn't. In fact, I'm willing to bet that Michael Hancock is dead. He had no hand in Ellen Cartwright's death, but his actions in helping get Pitman off the hook led indirectly to Norman Cartwright suicide, and to Ingrid's mental health problems."

Storm arrived with the drinks, and began to set them on the table. Joe watched him for a moment, then asked, "Where do you live, Storm?"

"I have a flat on—"

"Wastwater Street," Joe interrupted.

"Yes. How did you know?"

"Rott just told us." Ignoring surprised stares from Rott, Sheila, Brenda and Inspector Perry, Joe went on to ask, "And how's your mother?"

Storm shrugged, and placing the final drink before the policewoman, said, "I'm sorry, Mr Murray, but my mother passed away."

"I know she did, son. About a year ago. Overdose, wasn't it?"

Storm's colour drained. "I, er... well, yes as a matter of fact."

Joe nodded. "The very last person alive who could confirm that your real name is Orkan Cartwright."

# Chapter Fifteen

Joe's announcement was greeted with wide eyes and gasps from the people around them. Everyone turned on the barman and for a moment Joe thought Storm would deny it. But he did not. Instead, he placed his tray on a table nearby and sat down between Darlene and Cheryl.

He reached across and picked up Jezz's beer. "May I?" Jezz nodded and Storm took a sip before passing it back to Darlene's brother. He eyed Joe. "How did you know?"

Nelson had been hovering at the bar, clearly intent on listening in. Joe signalled to them. "Get him a soft drink."

Nelson hurried behind the bar to obey.

Joe took a swallow from his glass. "I don't like coincidences. I know they happen all the time, but when I get too many happening all at once, then it spells planning, not coincidence." He smiled at Storm. "It was a clever set up, son, but when you're trying to hide yourself and your identity, there are some basic essentials, one of which is keep your mouth shut." Joe's gaze swung on Darlene. "Both of you."

"What are you on about, Joe?" Perry demanded.

"Storm wouldn't tell me why he was so named. He said it was to do with his birthday and I should be able to guess it because I knew his star sign. Libra. It covers the back half of September and the first half of October. Now bear in mind that the Cartwright son was sixteen years old at the time of Ellen's murder and the father's suicide. What famous event did we have in October, sixteen years earlier? The hurricane. Remember it? He was born on the night of the fifteenth, sixteenth of October, the night of the hurricane, and in order to remind themselves, his parents named him Orkan: hurricane in Danish."

"Swedish, actually," Storm said. "My mother's parents were from Helsingborg."

"Whatever. He arrived here about a year ago. Now ask yourself what are the chances of Adam Pitman turning up from an area where he's suspected of a murder to an area where the murder victim's brother was living just by coincidence? Pretty remote, I'd say. Next, what are the chances of old Ma Cartwright dying, Michael Hancock disappearing and her son and Darlene Garbutt turning up here all at about that same time? Again it's so remote, you'd never get the bookie to give you a price on coincidence. But they might have got away with it, if it hadn't been for Rott's keys, which is what just put the seal on it." He smiled at Darlene. "Neat piece of work that. Worm your way into Rott's bed to nick his keys." Turning to Perry, he said, "There was no other way they could have got into the van. Wes told us last night and Rott has just said so. He also said he hadn't been burgled, so the only way anyone could have got the keys was by being in Rott's place at his invitation."

Alarm spread quickly across Darlene's face. She looked to Storm to help, but he sat calm, quiet and composed.

Nelson delivered a glass of lemonade to the young man, and waited. Slowly everyone else's attention came that way, too.

Storm took a sip and cleared his throat. "If you're waiting for me to say I'm sorry, and I didn't mean it, you'll wait a long time. I intended to kill him. I meant it and I'm not sorry. He murdered my sister, and the police had him. All along they promised us justice, and what happened? That crooked cop helped get him off. My father was an honest, decent, hard working man, and he couldn't take it, so he hanged himself. My mother had lost her beautiful daughter, and then she lost

170

the only man who was ever important to her. She was left with a young son, withdrawn into his shell, shocked by all that had happened, and her mind snapped. Between them, Pitman and Hancock cut short my sister's life, and my father's, and ruined my mother's life and mine. They deserved everything they got."

A stiff silence fell. Joe drank more lemonade. "Right. Yeah. All right, Storm. Take us back to the beginning. Why did Pitman murder your sister?"

The young man shrugged. "We never really knew. Hancock said it was drugs. Pitman was a dealer. Middle man. Not street level. He supplied the street men. If Ellen was on drugs, we didn't know about it. He got away with it because Hancock was taking a back hander. But he did murder Ellen. Even the cops knew it. He was banged to rights on it, and looking at a life sentence. He had only one way out."

"Detective Sergeant Hancock," Perry said.

Storm nodded. "I don't know how he managed it, but he got to speak to Hancock alone during one of his interviews."

"Recorders could have been switched off if another officer needed a bathroom break, or something," Perry said. "Go on."

"No matter how he managed it, he made it plain to Hancock what would happen if he went down. Hancock would be going with him. There was some negotiating, and they came to a deal. Hancock would make changes to Pitman's statement. Nothing major. Just enough to cast doubt on it. The courts would then be challenged on the accuracy of the entire police case. Hancock knew it would be the end of his career, but it was easier than ending his career and serving fifteen years for corruption. But he cut himself a good deal. Pitman would introduce him to importers. Hancock would become a middle man, just like Pitman. He would be making twice, three times what he could earn as a detective. Hancock bought it, and the rest you know. Pitman was acquitted on the judge's order. We complained, we got up a campaign for a retrial, but the CPS refused to open the case again."

"They would have needed fresh evidence," Perry said, "and if it wasn't forthcoming, they wouldn't risk hundreds of thousands, possibly millions of pounds on a trial they couldn't win."

Storm glared. "And that's what it comes down to, does it? Money? What is the value of my sister's life, my father's life, my mother's sanity?" He picked up his glass and drank again. When he next spoke, he was much calmer. "The police even let Hancock off with nothing worse than the sack. They said his actions were misguided but in good faith, so they fired him. Afterwards, they never even nailed him for drugs. He and Pitman were laughing at the law, laughing at us, laughing all the way to the bank, and I was nursing my broken mother and I got madder and madder and madder." He licked his lips and had to lubricate his throat again. "So I decided if the law couldn't give us justice, I'd have to take it. Both of them would pay for what they'd done. Hancock first, then Pitman."

"Why that way round?" Joe asked.

"Because I needed to know what Hancock knew," Storm replied. "I needed to know what Pitman had on him. I met with Hancock in a derelict warehouse down by the river. He was cocky, sure of himself. When I threatened to go to the police with what I knew about him, he laughed, told me to do it, but he also said I wouldn't live twenty-four hours after opening my mouth. We argued, he came at me, but I was carrying a crowbar. I hit him with it, broke his leg. I heard it crack." Storm smiled. "He was in agony. I threatened to smash his head in if he didn't tell me everything. He did." He smiled again. "And I smashed his head in anyway. I dragged his body into a corner amongst some rubble. As far as I know it's still there."

Silence fell again. Joe broke it. "You'd got rid of Hancock, and then it was Pitman's turn? Right?"

Storm nodded. "Pitman was more difficult. He was more

careful than Hancock. It would be nearly impossible to get him to an empty warehouse on a deserted industrial estate. Not on his own, anyway. But I got lucky. I was in the Engine House one night and I saw him arguing with Darlene. I played it cool and gradually got to know her, and eventually she told me what was going on between them."

"He owed me money," Darlene said. "He paid me fifty quid for those skin shots I told you about, but he made thousands from them. I tried everything to get him to pay up. I even threatened to send Jezz and Ricky round, but he wouldn't pay."

"I came up with a plan," Storm said, taking up the narrative. "And it was simple enough. Darlene told me about her best friend from uni; Kelly. How she'd made it through teacher training and got herself a secure job here in her hometown. We would leave East London, move up here, and when the time was right, we'd tempt Pitman up here, off his turf, and I'd record him admitting everything. We'd take that to the cops and they'd have him."

"That kind of evidence wouldn't hold up in court," Joe said.

"I knew that all along, Mr Murray. Darlene didn't."

"Are you saying Darlene was not aware that you intended to kill Mr Pitman?" Perry asked.

Storm nodded. "As far as she was concerned, the plan was to trap him. Nothing more. She had no part in the killing. I am responsible for that."

"And my brothers knew nothing about it," Darlene assured them. "I brought them here as ushers. They were friends of Kelly's as well as my family."

"Not according to Kelly." Joe stared owlishly at the two men, and then concentrated on Storm. "There was the problem of your mother, though, wasn't there?" Joe pointed out.

Storm looked uncomfortable. "She had no life, Mr Murray. She was drugged during the day, drugged to help her sleep at night. Drugged, drugged, drugged. What kind of existence was that for her? As far I was concerned, ending her life was a mercy, not a crime."

"Her sleeping pills," Joe said. "Let me guess. Zolpidem."

Again Storm nodded. "It was simple enough for me to hold them back. She was prescribed two at night when needed. I gave her one and kept the others. By the time Darlene had joined Kelly up here and I was ready to leave London, I had enough for a lethal dose."

"According to your neighbours, you had disappeared some time before her death," Perry pointed out.

"And you think that's difficult to arrange?" Storm demanded. "What they really meant was they hadn't seen me for a while. I set that up. I never went out through the front door. I was careful to avoid them on the street or anywhere in the local area. And I was the one who called the police in a panic having seen my mother dead through the windows." He sneered. "Police? You think you're so smart, yet you were duped by twenty-three-year-old kid."

"And you followed Darlene up here," Joe said, bringing the debate back on track. "You had enough of the sleeping pills left for what you had in mind."

"And you're another one who thinks he's got all the answers," Storm snapped. "I had sleeping pills left, Murray. I didn't know what I would use them for because we hadn't put the whole plan into place at that time."

Joe wondered if he was the only one to notice he had come down from 'Mr Murray' to plain 'Murray' as Storm's irritation rose.

"So how did the plan come about?" he asked.

"Wes and Kelly," Storm said. "When Darlene told me she was to be Kelly's chief bridesmaid, the idea occurred to me. I couldn't think of anywhere better for Pitman to show up than at a wedding. There are lots of people at a wedding, people get drunk at a wedding, and there are always arguments at weddings."

"So you began texting Pitman, threatening to blow his real operation wide open."

Storm nodded. "I used an unregistered mobile, and really put the pressure on him. Then the coup de grace: posing as Darlene, I sent him a text warning him that I would be talking to the newspapers and the cops once I'd seen Wes and Kelly off on honeymoon. He bought it and turned up."

"Suppose he hadn't?" Joe demanded. "Suppose he ignored you? Suppose he sent someone else? What then?"

Storm shrugged. "He didn't, but if he had, I'd have just kept the pressure on him. And so what if he had sent some of his hard cases instead? You think Jezz, Ricky, Paul and Wes couldn't have dealt with them? It's irrelevant. He showed up, and that was all we needed. Darlene urged Paul to help, Jezz and Ricky got involved. You even got involved." He laughed again. "Absolute magic."

"You even told him to check into the Waterside, didn't you?"

"I work down there most night, so what better way to keep tabs on him," Storm agreed.

"And then you fed Rott the sleeping pills, and texted Pitman to meet you, didn't you?"

Storm nodded slowly. "Darlene fed Paul the pills, as it happens. But she didn't take any. She needed to stay awake to make sure Paul didn't. I sent Pitman another message, again posing as Darlene, telling him to meet my representative at the old boat shed. My man would be alone, he had to be alone, too, or my man would walk away. No hassle, no negotiation. A final settlement. I knew he'd get there early. I was dressed in Rott's overalls and I watched him from the boat station as he wandered off towards the old shed. I gave him a few minutes and followed. He was taking pictures near the shed when I got there, and do you know something. He didn't even recognise me. He murdered my sister and he didn't even realise who I was. Christ, that made my blood boil even more." Storm paused a moment, took another sip of lemonade and made a visible effort to calm down. "There was a bit of two way chat and threats, me talking for Darlene, playing the innocent messenger boy, him threatening her with visits from his 'friends' if she didn't lay off. Then I told him that according to Darlene, his good friend Sergeant Hancock was dead. He laughed and said he didn't give a… well you know. While he was laughing, I pulled the pipe wrench out of the overalls, and smashed it down on his head. It all happened so fast, he didn't have time to scream. I hit him again just to make sure he was dead, then took off his camera strap, wrapped it round his throat and hung him from one of the boat hooks."

"You dumped the wrench in the lake," Joe pointed out, "but you smashed up his camera and dropped that in, too. Why? Had he taken pictures of you?"

"Not sure," Storm said. "He might have done. I wasn't willing to take the chance. I also threw the mobile phones in the lake; mine and his. I dropped the wrench in close to the shore where it would be easy to find, and I threw both the camera and phones further out. They'll probably turn up one day, but they'll be useless."

"We don't need them." Perry said. "As a matter of routine, we would get records of his mobile phone. The texts will show up."

"The times and date, yes, but not the content," Storm said.

"Just get back to the boathouse" Joe insisted. "You killed him. What then?"

"Nothing," Storm said. "I dumped the overalls, and came back here." He laughed once more. "I carried on serving booze to you all, watching you run round like headless chickens. It was wonderful. I would have called the cops, but I didn't need to. I think someone on the lake must have seen us fighting, or maybe they saw his body hanging."

"The latter," Perry confirmed.

"And it was you who rang Wes and Rott to complain about a gas leak," Joe said.

"Easy. I lived opposite. Call them to a house where the only parking place would leave the van out of their sight for a minute or two while they argued on the door with the old moaner who lives there. It was long enough for me to get into the van, using the keys Darlene supplied, steal the overalls and the pipe wrench."

Joe's anger, which had been rising throughout the tale, began to pour out. "You were quite content to let Rott take the blame for your crime. So what happened to all this bull about simply avenging your sister's death? What happened to the great vigilante act? If you were so determined to extract justice, you'd want everyone to know about it."

"And spend the rest of my life in prison? I don't think so."

"Pull the other one," Joe retorted. He rounded on Darlene. "And you, young lady. You didn't know he was going to kill Pitman? So how did he explain the pipe wrench he nicked with the overalls? He was planning a bit of DIY?"

"I didn't see the wrench," Darlene protested. "He had it wrapped in the overalls."

"I told you. Darlene thought we were just trying to trap him."

Joe gave them a solitary round of applause. "Bravo, bravo. Author, author."

Everyone looked at him as if he had taken leave of his senses. Only Storm said so.

"Have you lost your marbles?"

"No, lad, I've found them. It's a remarkable story, but that's all it is."

Anger suffused the young man's features. "Everything I've just told you is the truth."

"Some of it may well be, but I think most of it is a fallback against the danger of someone like me rumbling you." Joe got to his feet. "Stand up."

Puzzled, Storm obeyed.

Joe spoke to the rest of his small audience. "Now look at us. I'm five feet six in my stockinged feet and I weigh about nine stones. Storm isn't much taller than me, but I guess he weighs a lot less. Now even if he wrapped the camera strap round Pitman's throat first, how could he lift Pitman's body off the floor and hang it on that hook? My job keeps me pretty fit, and I have enough strength for what I need to do in life, but for a something like that I'd need someone to help me: someone taller and stronger." His eye fell on his nephew. "Someone like Lee or Rott."

"It weren't me, Uncle Joe," Lee protested.

"And I'm getting fed up of people blaming me," Rott complained.

"I know it wasn't you, Lee, and I know you were out for the count, Rott. We know what Wes was up to so that leaves only one candidate… Correction; *two* candidates." His gaze shifted quickly and fell on Jezz and Ricky.

The two brothers looked at each other and then bolted.

Rott stuck out a foot and tripped Jezz before he could get three feet. Ricky made it past Lee, but Joe's nephew jumped up, ran after him and brought him down with a waist-high tackle by the exit just as a team of police officers, led by Constable Lesney, stepped in.

"Good to know I've still gorrit," Lee said, getting to his feet. His face split into a broad grin as he yanked Ricky up.

With the brothers restrained and marched back to the table, Joe continued his analysis.

"Brenda cracked this part of it for me last night."

"I did?" Brenda grinned. "How?"

"You said I was a shortarse who couldn't reach the top pie racks."

"Well you can't," Sheila said.

"Correct, and as I just listened to Storm I realised that he's a shortarse, too. He couldn't reach the top pie racks, either, and

178

he couldn't reach that hook in the old boathouse. At least not while he was lifting up Pitman's body, he couldn't. But the camera strap was too short to hook on from the floor, especially if it was wrapped round Pitman's neck at the time. So whoever did it must have lifted the dead man up. Therefore, it wasn't Storm."

"Logical," Perry agreed. "So what the hell has been going on?"

"I'm gonna speculate and say a takeover bid," Joe replied. "Think about the manner in which Pitman got his acquittal. He got a hooky cop to alter the evidence. Storm doesn't know any hooky cops, other than, maybe, Hancock, but I'll guarantee that Hancock is dead. I'll also guarantee that his body is at the bottom of the Thames and not in the warehouse where Storm claims it to be. So what happens next? You, Inspector, charge him and the CPS bring the case to court. In the meantime some of the anomalies begin to show up and Storm's statement is exposed as a farce. When pressed, he will claim that Pitman's people threatened him, forced him to confess. They even killed his mad mother to press home their point. But what's really happening? Storm is hell bent on killing Pitman, and it's probably true that what Pitman did to his family is part of the motive, but his real intention is to take over Pitman's East London turf. While Storm is inside for trying to pervert the course of justice, Darlene and her two brothers are marking out the territory with the cocaine stolen from Pitman's bags."

Perry was nonplussed. "We found traces, Joe, not a stash."

"Because he'd already taken the stash," Joe argued, pointing the finger at Storm. "Maddy Chester told me he was working at the Waterside on Thursday and he was there again yesterday. And the real reason Pitman turned up at the wedding and at the boat station was he wanted his dope back." To Perry, he went on, "Check the flat in Wastwater Street. Check Jezz and Ricky's room. Check their cars. I guarantee you'll find it."

Perry glanced around the four suspects. "Do any of you have anything to say?"

When they did not respond, she nodded to Lesney. "Read them their rights and charge them, Constable."

Flanked by uniformed officers, Storm stood and delivered a menacing glare of pure hatred on Joe. "One day, they'll let me out. And when they do, I'll come looking for you."

Joe smiled. "Lazy Luncheonette, Doncaster Road, Sanford. You can't miss it." He jerked a thumb at Lee. "It's where my giant nephew works."

***

Lee lifted the last suitcase into the car, and as his nephew backed off to return to his own car, Joe slammed the tailgate to lock the luggage in.

Nelson and Harriet Atkinson stood nearby.

"I do hope these unfortunate events haven't put you off the Lake District and The Lakeside Manor Hotel, Mr Murray," Nelson simpered. "We'd love to have you as our guests again."

"With a new pair of shorts, one hopes," said Harriet, sternly.

"There you go, you see," Joe replied. "I spend so much money on classy hotels like yours I can't afford new shorts." He shook hands with them both. "It's been an interesting weekend. Thanks for everything."

While the hotel managers returned to their work, Joe prepared to climb into the car, and as he did so, Perry's silver-grey Vauxhall drove into the car park and stopped nearby.

"Just wanted to say thanks for your help, Joe," she said as she climbed out.

"No problem. Have you searched their flat?"

The inspector nodded and said, "You were right. We found traces of cocaine in the place and Scientific Support will tell us whether it comes from the same batch as we found in Pitman's room. They're still ripping the place apart looking for the alleged stash, and if it's there, we'll find it. If not, the Met will look at the Garbutt brothers' place." She sighed. "Like you, I think young Cartwright started out with lofty ambitions, but somewhere along the line, he realised there was a good profit to be made, if he could break into it, and taking Pitman's merchandise would provide the foothold he needed. Even if he tries to retract his confession to murder, we should still get him on attempting to pervert the course of justice, and possession with intent to supply."

"What about Darlene?"

Perry frowned. "Bit more difficult. She insists she's innocent of anything other than helping him in a plot to coerce Pitman into a confession."

"And her brothers?" Joe asked.

"Both Jezz and Ricky are saying nothing."

Joe opened his car door and prepared to get in. "You'll keep me posted?"

"Absolutely. I have your number." They shook hands. "You know, Joe, you would have made a brilliant police officer. How come you never joined?"

He laughed and got behind the wheel. "My dad needed someone to run the caff after my brother went to Australia."

"He's lying," Sheila called out from the passenger seat. "When he applied, there was a height restriction and he wasn't tall enough."

"In other words," Brenda echoed, "he's too short a shortarse. I told you. He can't even reach the top pie racks in the Lazy Luncheonette kitchen."

Joe grinned at the inspector, closed his door and let down the window. Turning the key in the ignition, he smiled out at Perry. "I'll see you around sometime." He fired the engine, slotted the car into gear, and drove away. "Another weekend brought to a satisfactory conclusion."

"Not quite, Joe," Brenda said from the back seat. "You

promised to stop smoking and see the doctor."

As they wound their way along the lane, Joe shook his head and lit a cigarette and controlled the desperate urge to cough. "I said I'd see the doctor and I promised to *try* and stop smoking."

Sheila smiled. "And we're there to make sure you do try, Joe."

# Chapter Sixteen

On Monday morning, the hot weather had given way to the promised thundery showers, but to Joe's delight, the morning had been as busy as any other day, with most of the draymen glad to see him back and their favourite breakfast eatery open for business.

As he had promised, Joe made an appointment with his GP, and after a debate with the receptionist, during which he insisted the matter was urgent, he had cut along at eleven in the morning. With the time coming up to noon, and the lunchtime rush under way, he returned, but it was two in the afternoon before they finally sat at table five for a well-earned rest and he could bring them fully up to date.

"That doctor is an idiot," Joe declared. "He swears blind he's been telling me to stop smoking for years, when I know for a fact I haven't seen him for five years."

"So what did he say, Joe?" Sheila asked.

"He tested my breathing with this thing. A Spirograph or something."

"Spirometer," Brenda corrected.

"Probably. I had to puff my breath into it half a dozen times."

"And what was the outcome?"

Joe's face fell. "My lungs are shot. COPD. Cash on prearranged delivery."

"Chronic obstructive pulmonary disease." Sheila sounded triumphant. "Just as Inspector Perry suggested."

"It's incurable," Brenda said.

"It's a measure of lung efficiency," Joe told them, "not a bloody death sentence."

"It's still incurable," Brenda insisted, "and if you don't pack the weed in, Joe, it will kill you before your time."

"So he says. But what the hell does he know?"

"He's a doctor."

"He's a bone idle git," Joe retorted. "And he smokes a bloody pipe. Cheeky sod."

"Pipes are thought not to be as bad," Sheila ventured. "Has he done anything other than give you advice?"

Joe dug into his pocket and came out with an inhaler. "Salbutamol sulphate. One puff as and when needed. It'll help when I get breathless."

Brenda laughed wickedly. "You'll need a good few puffs before you climb into bed with me again, then."

With a grimace of disapproval at her friend, Sheila changed the subject. "And talking of Inspector Perry, have you heard anything yet?"

Joe yawned and nodded. "She rang at half past eleven, just as I came out of the doc's. Did I not tell you?"

"No. You didn't."

"When she got back to the station yesterday, she went over the preliminary pathology report on Pitman's body. There were no fingerprints, so whoever moved him to hang him up was wearing gloves. But there were marks on the body, made by their hands, and they were way too large for Storm's mitts. She called the pathologist out, got some measurements and they fitted Jezz's hands perfectly. As of last night, they still hadn't admitted it, but it was Jezz who strung him up, probably with Ricky's help."

Brenda frowned. "So what were Storm and Darlene doing all this time?"

"Perry thinks Storm was with them, but it'll be tough to prove. The CCTV from the boat station is a bit grainy, but the man seen wearing Rott's overalls is too small for them. They

184

hang on him like a loose sack of spuds. Perry believes it was Storm. In the meantime, the search teams went into their place on Wastwater Street, and they found a large stash of cocaine in the water tank. Finally, just as I guessed, she contacted the Met and they went to the warehouse in East London, looking for Hancock's remains and found nothing. There's another inquiry into that, but she reckons the same as I did. He's dead and at the bottom of the Thames. All in all, it's gonna be difficult to prove, but they'll get something on all of them."

"But Storm killed his mother," Brenda protested.

"That was another lie," Joe said with a shake of the head. "He was working the day his mother died. He actually came home and found her dead. That's when he disappeared. She died of an overdose, true, but it wasn't Zolpidem. She couldn't take them because she was on antidepressants. She took about fifty paracetemol, and there was nothing to suggest anyone else was involved. The Zolpidem were actually prescribed for Storm, not her. He had the whole thing worked out perfectly. If Perry had accepted his story yesterday, he would get off on the mangled evidence, and then serve, maybe, two years for attempting to pervert the course of justice. He could even end up with a suspended sentence, but at the worst, he'd be out in a year, and then he would join Darlene and her brothers leading the high life, probably somewhere on the continent."

"What I don't understand is why go to all this trouble in the first place," Sheila said. "It wasn't as though anyone suspected him until you rumbled it, Joe."

"I told you yesterday, it was a fallback plan. It was there just in case anyone did put it together." Joe grunted. "I guess he didn't expect someone like me to rumble it so early."

Brenda sighed. "That Pitman was an evil man. So was Sergeant Hancock. But Storm was just as bad, really, wasn't he?"

"Every bit as bad if you want my opinion," Joe replied. He

finished off his tea. "Better make a start on cleaning down, eh? Knock off early for a change."

"Hear, hear," Sheila agreed. "I have to say, Joe, when it comes to crime, you're a genius."

"Yes, well, the impossible, I can do."

"He's a genius who doesn't smoke anymore," Brenda applauded.

"But miracles might take a bit longer."

## THE END

TURN THE PAGE
TO READ THE FIRST CHAPTER
OF THE NEXT STAC MYSTERY,
COSTA DEL MURDER...

# Costa del Murder

## Chapter One

Flashing blue lights cut through the rainy September night. The ambulance braked for a set of lights on red, the driver checked both ways and accelerated through the junction, the siren wowing to warn other vehicles off.

In the back, Joe Murray lay strapped onto a trolley, an oxygen mask covering his nose and mouth. His breathing came in painful gasps and his left arm hurt. Unable to speak (and even if he could he would never make himself heard through the mask) he silently thanked God for the impulse that had made him give Brenda and Sheila keys to not only the Lazy Luncheonette but his upstairs apartment, too. Without them, they would not have raised the alarm until tomorrow morning when they couldn't get in. They would have called the emergency services who would have broke in and would have found him... dead.

The word rang round his head. It couldn't be happening. Not to him. Fifty-six was no age to hang up his teapot and hand in his whites.

But there was no mistaking the symptoms. Chest pains, spreading to his left arm, sweating, struggling to breathe and when he did catch his breath it was shallow and painful.

Heart attack!

"Brenda, help me," he had croaked into his mobile. "I'm dying."

Brenda Jump had known him long enough to know when he was not pulling her leg, not simply seeking a sympathetic ear. Giving him instructions to stay still and calm, she rang the ambulance from home, then jumped in her car and drove to the Lazy Luncheonette, arriving there a few minutes ahead of the paramedics. Somewhere along the line, she also rang Sheila Riley, their friend and fellow employee, and she arrived just after the ambulance.

By then, Joe had begun to feel better, but the paramedics were taking no chances. They checked his pulse and temperature, and ran an ECG. They even pricked his thumb and checked his blood sugar despite his protests that he was not diabetic. Talking over the phone to a doctor in A & E, they eventually strapped him to the gurney and hauled him down the stairs and into the waiting ambulance, where Brenda climbed in the back with him while Sheila followed in her car.

And while he lay bound to the trolley, Brenda gave the paramedic, a young woman named Karen, his details, and Joe thought about mortality.

How could this be happening? He was fifty-six, not eighty-six. He had never been overweight in his life, and his work kept him reasonably fit. People of his age and general good health didn't have heart attacks.

The truth hit him like a hammer. Men his age did have heart attacks. Not often, but they did. Men his age died from them. Not often, but they did. Gripped by the fear of approaching eternity, the thought sent his pulse racing again.

While the ambulance hurtled along the roads, he thought about all the things he had meant to do before he died, and regrettably, discovered that they did not amount to much. He had achieved almost everything he wanted in his half century and a bit, and the things he had wanted badly would never come anyway. Like joining the police force. He had always been too short, and by the time they removed the height restriction he was too old.

And while he thought about his thin, unfulfilled ambitions, the question rapped repeatedly at his brain. Why me, why me, why me? What had he ever done that he deserved to die at such a young age?

The ambulance screamed into the A & E parking area, the back doors flew open, Karen and her driver unhitched the trolley, and hurried him down the ramp. Briefly exposed to the chilly, wet, night, he shivered, but then he was inside the hospital, zooming along under the overhead lighting, the bland walls of the corridor rushing past him on both sides.

When they stopped, he could hear them talking about him.

"Male, fifty-six. Presenting chest pains, left arm pains. Pulse irregular, breathing laboured."

"Leave him with us."

The paramedics disappeared. A young man, wearing the dark blue jumper of a hospital porter, appeared behind his head and began to wheel him along. Brenda hurried alongside him, holding his hand, trying to reassure him.

They spun the trolley round, pushed him into a cubicle. A nurse appeared, slipping her hands into protective gloves, preparing a cannula.

"Are you his wife, luv?"

"What? Oh, God, no. I'm a close friend and an employee. Getting in touch with his next of kin is, er, problematic. She lives in Tenerife."

Joe wanted to protest that Alison was no longer his next of kin, but the nurse was too busy to listen.

She leaned over him, a reassuring smile on her pretty face. "Just a little scratch, Joe."

He felt the sting of the needle bite into the back of his hand, and the cannula slide into the vein. Then came the fumbling discomfort of the nurse strapping it to the back of his hand.

"We really should have his next of kin, you know, Mrs...?"

Again he wanted to complain, but they were taking little

notice of him.

"Jump. Brenda Jump. There's nowt about Joe Murray that I can't tell you. I've known him fifty years or more. The nearest he has to family in Sanford is his nephew, Lee, but we can't get him out of bed at this time of night. He has to open up in about four hours. After Lee, there's only Alison, and like I said, she lives in the Canary Islands."

Listening in on the conversation, Joe made a rapid calculation in his head. Four hours? Lee usually arrived at six. That meant it must be two in the morning.

"I can open up myself if you let me go," he shouted, but his words were muffled by the oxygen mask.

But at least this time he had their attention and the nurse removed the mask. "What did you say, Joe?"

"I said, if you stop buggering me about, I can open up the café myself."

"You can't go anywhere until you've been seen by a doctor," the nurse told him. "Now, do you want to give me all your details?"

He scowled. "Ask Brenda. She knows it all."

Sheila joined them soon after, but it was to be a long wait. The two women were sent out when the doctor, a young blonde woman who Joe was sure used to call into his café for soft drinks and snacks when she was a schoolgirl, examined him. They took another ECG, and more blood, and he was left waiting again.

Brenda and Sheila looked exhausted, and he felt waves of fatigue sweeping over him.

"Why don't you two go home?" he suggested. "I'll get a taxi back to the café."

"We're staying here, Joe," Sheila told him, "until we know how you are and what's happening."

Just after five in the morning, the doctor returned.

"Right, Mr Murray. We don't think you've had a heart attack, but we're not sure, so we're keeping you in."

"No way. I'm going home now."

Joe tried to swing his legs off the trolley, but Brenda stopped him.

"Use your nut, Joe, and stay where you are."

"I have to be there—"

"So you can drop dead while we're serving the draymen?" Sheila asked. "We'll be so busy delivering breakfasts we won't have time to pick you up. The café will survive without you for a day or two. Stay where you are."

"I can't leave it to Lee—"

"He manages when we're away, Joe, so he can manage now," Sheila insisted. "I'll ring Lee in half an hour and make sure he knows. He'll bring Cheryl and her friends in, and the Lazy Luncheonette will survive. Now stop behaving like a child and stay where you are."

Sheila's words forced another memory into his mind. Her husband, Peter, a personal friend of Joe's had been barely fifty years old when a double heart attack killed him.

He pointed at the doctor who had been listening to the exchange. "She just said I hadn't had a heart attack."

"No, Mr Murray, I said we don't think you've had a heart attack. We're not sure. We need to carry out a second blood test twelve hours after the first." She checked her watch. "That's about two o'clock in the afternoon. Your breathing is poor. Your chest is clacking like a rattlesnake in a bad mood. There may be some kind of infection in there. Now for your own good we're keeping you in. Once we have the results of the second bloods, we'll know more and we can think about letting you go home, but there'll be no work for a while, so get used to it."

Joe flopped back onto the trolley. There was nothing else to do.

\*\*\*

It was twelve fifteen in the early afternoon when Sheila and Brenda met in Ma's Pantry, their favourite café in The Gallery shopping centre.

"Les said he would be here for about half past," Brenda reported.

"I rang the hospital half an hour ago," Sheila said. "They say Joe's fine, but grumpy, and would we please give them permission to put him to sleep… permanently."

Brenda chuckled, and stirred her latte. "Never changes, does he?" Her face became more serious. "What will we do without him, Sheila? You know, if…"

"That was a question I asked myself so many times after Peter died. How will I survive without him?" She smiled brightly. "But I did. I don't think it's an issue with Joe, though. You'll see. He'll be back in no time, moaning at us." Again she frowned. "But if it really isn't a heart attack, what is it?"

"Lifestyle." Brenda's firm tones brooked no argument. "You know, he's stressed to hell most of the time running the Lazy Luncheonette. He dashes about like a blue-arsed fly, trying to do everything, and even when he finishes, he spends hours doing the books and working out the orders for the following day. Then there are those bloody cigarettes. How many times have we asked him to stop smoking? How much grief did I give him at Windermere during the summer? He doesn't eat properly, either. The only time he gets a decent, proper meal is when he comes to your house, mine or goes to Lee's on a Sunday. The rest of the week, he lives on snacks, and microwave dinners."

Sheila chewed her lip. "And if he's not working on the café, he's fiddling with bits for the 3rd Age Club. What he needs is de-stressing." A sly smile crossed her face. "Shall we send him off to Tenerife to be with Alison?"

"What a good idea." Brenda laughed again. "First off, let's sort the club out with Les, then we can cut along to the travel agent's and see what they might have on offer." Her face took

194

on the appearance of someone who's just had an idea. "How would you fancy a week in the sun?"

"Ooh, not half. You me and Joe. We can keep an eye on him, make sure he gets plenty of rest."

"And raid his wallet for goodies."

A look of serious intent spread across Sheila's features. "Not Tenerife, though. I was joking about that. I don't think mixing with Alison would do him any good."

"Fine with me. There are plenty of places on mainland Spain with vacancies at this time of year. Or we could look at the Balearics."

Sheila began to get excited. "I haven't been to Majorca since before Peter died."

Brenda was about to answer, but caught sight of Les Tanner's imposing figure making towards them. "Here comes the captain."

Les, a former Captain in the Territorial Army Reserve, greeted them cordially, joined them, and after securing a cup of tea and a cheese sandwich, listened to the tale of Joe's overnight adventures.

"Always said it would be the death of him one day, that café. I'm surprised he hasn't handed the reins over to Lee before today. Taken a bit of a back seat. What do the medics say?"

"Nothing definite yet, Les," Sheila replied. "They don't think it's a heart attack, but they won't know for sure until later this afternoon."

"Whatever it is," Brenda told him, "Joe is going to need some rest, so we need someone to take over the running of the 3rd Age Club while he's down. You were the natural choice."

"Glad you think so, Brenda." Les beamed at her. "And of course, I'd be delighted. Y'know, I've had my share of clashes with Murray, but they've never been personal. Wouldn't like to see any harm come to him. First order of business will be to organise a get well message from the members to our

Chairman." He bit into his sandwich, chewed and swallowed. "So what will you do with him? Sit him at a corner table in the Lazy Luncheonette and make him do crosswords all day?"

"We were just discussing that, Les," Sheila said. "We're going to the travel agent's when we leave here. We're thinking of taking him to Spain for a week or two."

"Good idea. Bit of sun and sand. Just the thing after a wobbler." Les swallowed a mouthful of tea. "Look, I don't want to sound pushy or anything, but Sylvia and I have an apartment in Spain."

The two women exchanged smirks. "Do you now?"

"Yes, Brenda, we do." Les appeared at his most imperiously disapproving. "Our relationship is an open secret, you know."

"Yes, Les, we know," Sheila agreed. "What were you saying about an apartment in Spain?"

"It's in a complex on the Costa del Sol. There's a pool, lawns, patio area. Ideal place for a little R and R."

"Oh, that's good of you, Les," Brenda said. "How much?"

"On the house," Les replied. "With my compliments. Lest I can do for the miserable old so-and-so."

Sheila appeared concerned. "Are you sure, Les? I mean we don't object to paying our way."

"Wouldn't hear of it. I pay the rent monthly from my bank. All you need is your flight, and you can get a return to Malaga for less than a hundred pounds."

The two women exchanged glances again.

"You'll need to arrange a transfer from Malaga Airport, but it's only about twenty minutes away. You can get a taxi for less than fifteen euros."

Sheila said, "It sounds like a bargain."

"It's agreed, then. I'll ring the apartment supervisor and let him know to expect you on Monday."

\*\*\*

196

Dr McKay, a tall, gangly man in his late thirties, perched on the edge of the bed, where he could face Joe and his two companions.

"There's good news and bad news, Joe. The good news is, you haven't had a heart attack. The bad news is, you're high on the waiting list for one and it'll hit sooner rather than later if you don't watch it."

"I don't understand." Joe replied. "I take pretty good care of myself."

"That's a different tale to the one your friends here, tell me," McKay retorted. "We think, Joe, that this is muscle strain. You've probably lifted something too heavy, a little too high and pulled a muscle in your chest wall."

"We've warned him about lifting those trays of pies onto the top rack, doctor," Sheila said. "He's not really tall enough."

"That's why Lee is in the kitchen," Brenda said. "Young, big, strong as an ox."

"And daft as a brush," Joe pointed out.

"If he's there, you should be using him no matter how daft he is," McKay said. "You're overdoing it. You will get better, but only with rest."

"Right." Joe threw back the sheets. "Is that it? Can I go now?"

"Oh, whoa. Not so fast, my friend. I said the muscle strain will get better, but you have other problems, and they need some attention. Your breathing, for example. When were you first told to stop smoking?"

Joe had no hesitation. "About forty years ago. Not long after I first started."

"That attitude will get you nowhere, Joe," McKay told him. "Now come on. How long has your breathing bothered you?"

"I don't know, do I? Three, four years. It's got worse this last few months."

"We had a weekend in the Lake District during the summer, doctor," Sheila said, "and he was warned then about his breathing. He's already diagnosed with COPD."

"It doesn't bother me that much," Joe complained.

"It's killing you." McKay announced. "There's something else going on in there, too. An infection probably, so I'm prescribing an antibiotic. Amoxicillin, five hundred milligrams. One three times a day, and make sure you complete the seven day course. When that's done, go back to your doctor, ask him to repeat the spirometry test to check your breathing hasn't deteriorated. Next on the agenda, stress. I've been talking to your two lady friends here, Joe, and they've told me more than you did. You're under a lot of stress almost all the time."

"I'm a businessman. It goes with the territory."

"So it does, but it shouldn't be killing you and it is. You need some downtime. Let your accountant do the tax returns. Let the bank worry about your money. Let your staff do the lion's share of the work in the café. And finally, stop, bloody, smoking."

"Oh come on, Doc. I mean—"

"No, Joe. No excuses. Pack the weed in because if you don't, that croaky chest of yours will stop giving you enough oxygen and the heart attack will happen. Now I'm going to write to your GP with a few recommendations. I suspect there may be a touch of angina, so I'm going to recommend a coronary angiogram, over and above the spirometry. He needs to look at your blood pressure too. It's not seriously high, but it's higher than it should be. I want to see you in outpatients three months from now to see how you're getting on. All right?"

"No, Doc, it's not all right. I don't need all this faffing about. So I have a bad chest. It's these damp days and stupid bloody laws that make me go outside for a smoke. I'll take a few less cigarette breaks. I'll make these two lift the pies into the oven if that keeps you happy. Right now, all I want to do is go home."

"No, Joe. You will stop smoking and you will take it a bit easier. If you don't, the next thing these girls will have to think about will be your funeral." McKay looked to the two women for support.

"Don't worry, Doctor. We'll make him do as he's told," Brenda promised.

McKay smiled. "Good. That's what I like to hear. Joe, this has been a shot across the bows. Don't ignore it. Change before it's too late. Take a few bob out of your hoards of cash and take a good, long, boring holiday." He stood up. "All right. You can go. Don't forget to pick up your prescription at the pharmacy on your way out."

McKay left, and Joe rolled off the bed. "Bloody quack. He ought to be struck off."

"He's giving you sound advice, Joe, and we're going to make sure you follow it."

"Ha. Are you? Let's wait and see, eh? I'll be back behind the counter first thing tomorrow morning."

The two women exchanged glances. "No you won't," Brenda said with a smile. "You'll be packing your cases."

"Would you two like to clear off for a minute while I get dressed…" He whirled on them. "What? What did you say?"

"First thing Monday morning, we drive over to Manchester," Sheila said. "We're on the seven fifteen flight for Malaga."

"What?"

"We're going to Torremolinos for a week, Joe," Brenda told him. "All three of us."

# Fantastic Books
# Great Authors

Meet our authors and discover our exciting
range:

- Gripping Thrillers
- Cosy Mysteries
- Romantic Chick-Lit
- Fascinating Historicals
- Exciting Fantasy
- Young Adult and Children's
  Adventures

Visit us at:
**www.crookedcatpublishing.com**

Join us on facebook:
**www.facebook.com/crookedcatpublishing**

Printed in Great Britain
by Amazon